DANNY ORLIS PLAYS HOCKEY

DANNY ORLIS PLAYS HOCKEY

BERNARD PALMER

Danny Orlis Plays Hockey
© 2023 by Bernard Palmer
All rights reserved. First edition 1957.
Second edition 2023.

Cover image: Adobe Firefly
Character illustrations: John Ball
Editor: Charlene Miskimen

Aneko Press *Youth*

www.anekopress.com

Aneko Press, Life Sentence Publishing, and our logos are trademarks of Life Sentence Publishing, Inc.
203 E. Birch Street
P.O. Box 652
Abbotsford, WI 54405

JUVENILE FICTION / Religious / Christian / Action & Adventure
Paperback ISBN: 978-1-62245-970-4
eBook ISBN: 978-1-62245-971-1
10 9 8 7 6 5 4 3 2
Available where books are sold

CONTENTS

CHAPTER 1

VOTED OUT

A bleak west wind was whipping the last of the fall leaves along the narrow Cedarton street and mixing them with snow. The clouds that had been floating across the horizon since early morning had finally blotted out the blue of the sky and were beginning to spit snow, faintly discernible against the dull gray of the buildings, but nonetheless obvious.

"We're going to be in for a real storm this time," Danny said to Kay as the two of them hurried along the sidewalk.

She shivered. "I almost wish I were back in Mexico."

"Let's go in here and have some ice cream. That'll warm you up."

"Not me," she said, going into the shop ahead of him. "I'm having hot chocolate."

Danny grinned at her.

When the waitress had taken their orders, Danny Orlis took a straw and held it between his fingers thoughtfully.

"My name's certainly 'mud' around this town," he said softly.

Kay looked up at him, the smile gone from her soft blue eyes.

"They'll forget about your not playing football before long."

"It isn't for myself that I care," he continued, "but I've been praying so hard for Kirk and some of the others. As long as they look down on me this way, there's no use trying to talk to them about the Lord."

"You settled all of that with God, Danny," Kay told him. "He'll help you work it out if you first trust."

Danny leaned forward intently. "I know that," he said, "and I think I know how He's going to do it. I'm going out for hockey tomorrow."

"But what about your work?"

"I've got most of my magazine customers lined up so I can work them Saturday mornings," he told her. "I don't have to worry about my job now."

The next afternoon after school was the first practice session of the hockey season, and the locker room was jammed with guys when Danny got his skates out of his coat locker and went downstairs.

The coach elbowed his way into the locker room and climbed up on a bench where he could be seen by everybody. "It's good to see so many of you out for the team," he said, smiling. "We've got some great prospects and we're going to have a fine team if you guys are willing to work."

He stopped and looked around. The smile left his face as he spied Danny.

"Aren't you in the wrong place, Orlis?" he demanded.

"I thought I'd try out for the team," Danny stammered.

"To tell you the truth, Orlis," Coach Masters retorted coldly, "I've never been much for a quitter."

"I don't intend to quit, sir."

"You quit in football," the coach snapped.

Danny flushed, but said nothing.

"This is something I'm going to have to put up to the guys," Coach Masters said. "It's no more than fair that they have a voice as to whether a guy who quit on them once gets another chance."

Danny gulped hard.

"Go up to my office, Orlis," the coach said. "I'll take the vote in a few minutes and tell you how it comes out."

The boy didn't answer him. He didn't dare trust his voice before the guys.

How long he was in the little office he didn't know, but finally Coach Masters opened the door and strode in.

"Well, the guys took their vote. It seems that they don't want you to play with them. They have no use for a quitter. I'd like to talk with you a minute, Orlis," he said.

There was a short silence.

"I'm sorry about the way the vote came out," Mr. Masters said. "But I knew how the guys felt, and I didn't want to start with dissension on the team."

"I can't say that I blame them," Danny managed.

Danny was supposed to see Kay that night to work on plans for a youth group party, but he couldn't – not after what happened. He checked out a book at the library so he could start reading for a book review and walked home alone through the snow and growing cold. He planned on going straight to his room as soon as he got home.

As he was taking off his coat, the phone rang. It was Kay.

"I've got to go over to the church and get some game books," she said, "and I wondered if you could come a little early so there'll be someone here when Rick and Marilyn get here. It's the first time we've ever been able to get them to agree to serve on a committee."

Rick Haines was one of the guys who had been out for hockey. He was one of those who had voted against him.

***

Marilyn spoke to Danny pleasantly enough, laughing and talking as she stomped the snow from her boots and slipped out of her heavy coat. But Rick smiled sarcastically and only grunted.

Kay came in just then and they all went over to the fireplace. They sat down on the floor in front of it and began to make plans for the youth group party.

"You'd better not start the party too early," Rick said. "Now that hockey practice has begun, most of the guys won't even get home from school until 6:30 or so. Most of the guys go out for hockey," Rick said significantly, staring directly at Danny, "but they don't all get to stay. We're a little particular about who plays with us."

Danny flushed scarlet.

The next morning Danny went to school a little early. He wanted to see the coach again.

"I thought we settled that matter last night," Mr. Masters said impatiently.

"We did," Danny told him, "but I just wondered if there'd be any chance of getting a job as student manager with the team. I could take care of the skates and look after the equipment and help dress down the ice and things like that."

The coach eyed him narrowly. "Do you mean to tell me," the instructor said, "that with the guys feeling like they do you'd still go down and wait on them as student manager?"

"Yes, sir," Danny replied.

"All I can say," the coach said, "is that you're a glutton for punishment."

The job as student manager of the hockey team was difficult and some of the guys did make it rough for him, but it gave him a chance to be on skates and to be around the game he had learned to enjoy back home on the Angle.

***

Tex was flying down from Baudette to take Danny and Kay to the Angle. Mrs. Orlis had insisted that the missionary girl spend Christmas with them. But Danny had him wait until the morning after school dismissed so he could help with the final hockey practice.

Not many of the guys showed up, but Coach Masters decided to go ahead with the scrimmage he had planned.

"And it may be," he said ominously, "that some of the varsity will find themselves on the second team when we get together after vacation."

When they lined up they were short a man to make two full teams. Coach Masters muttered something under his breath, then looked over at the sidelines where Danny was standing.

"All right, Orlis," he called. "Come on out here and play wing for the second team."

"You–you mean me?" Danny asked, as though he could scarcely believe his ears.

"How many guys named Orlis do we have?" the coach asked.

Danny grabbed up the nearest stick and skated out into position. "O Lord," he prayed silently, "help me to make good! Help me to make good!"

CHAPTER 2

A CHANCE AT HOCKEY

Danny skated over to the right wing position with the second team and crouched expectantly. This was it – the chance he had been waiting for – praying for. If only he could make good now! He looked up to see that Rick Haines was playing opposite him. The tall first team wing was fast and rough, a hard man to handle on the ice. And it had been a year ago Christmas since Danny had had a stick in his hands. It was going to be all he could do to keep within skating distance of the big regular.

Danny moistened his lips as the second team center skated to the middle of the rink.

"What do you think you're doing out here?" Rick asked Danny under his breath. "You don't think this means you're going to be able to worm your way in, do you?"

The color drained from Danny's face. That had been just what he had been thinking. Even then a prayer had been in his heart that God would help him to play good enough to make the team and Coach Masters reconsider.

The assistant coach, who was doubling as referee, skated out with the puck and the game began. The second team center managed to get control of the puck on the opening play and passed it to the other wing, who dribbled raggedly toward the sidelines. He shot a wobbly pass back to the center, who almost lost it as his man charged in. It was easy to see why they were on the second team. And yet they played savagely, as though they were playing in the dying moments of a conference game.

Danny faked Rick off balance, circled behind the center who was being closed in on from three directions, and took a clumsy backhanded pass. Instantly Danny came alive. He skated directly toward Rick, dribbling the puck close in front of him. The first team wing lunged forward, slashing with his stick, but Danny eluded him with a feint that sent him sprawling on the ice. He faked successfully, though somewhat clumsily, past the defense man and slapped the puck over the gaping goalie's stick into the net.

Coach Masters' whistle sounded raucously. "All right, Orlis," he bawled. "That's enough grandstanding. Don't you know you've got a team out there to help you?"

"Y-yes, sir," he stammered.

"Just remember that. If there's anything I can't stand it's a show-off," the instructor continued.

Danny started to speak, but stopped. What good would it do to argue?

Coach Masters turned to the defense man who played behind Danny, "You and Orlis change places, Bill," he said.

Rick Haines laughed impudently.

For the rest of the scrimmage Danny did the best he could, but his heart wasn't in the game. Every time he turned he could see the coach's pale blue eyes boring into him.

The next morning Danny was up at dawn wrapping the Christmas presents he had bought for his parents, the twins, and Kay and getting his bag packed. The clouds hung low and threatening, and there was a hint of snow in the chill December air.

"It doesn't make any difference to me what happens this Christmas," Mrs. Barber, his landlady, said sullenly. "We're not even going to have a tree or buy any presents for one another. We're going to act just as though Christmas wasn't even coming."

"Oh, but you've got to have some sort of Christmas, Mrs. Barber," Danny replied. "Christmas will mean a lot to Kirk this year, now that he's putting his trust in Christ."

"God doesn't think anything of me or the kids either."

"God doesn't promise to give us an easy life," Danny said, praying for wisdom. "He promises to give strength and help to meet what comes. Look at Kay. Her dad is dead and her mom is serving as a missionary down in Mexico. And the twins my parents adopted! They lost both their mom and dad. We ought to thank God for the wonderful blessings He has given us."

"God hasn't done anything for me," she muttered, brushing her hair back.

Danny didn't answer her immediately. Instead he opened his Testament to the Christmas story and read to her how Jesus had been born in a manger, how the angels proclaimed His coming and the shepherds came to worship Him.

"Jesus is God's gift to us, Mrs. Barber," Danny said softly. "And He gave His life for you and Kirk and Karen and me and anyone else who will accept His salvation."

She was weeping by this time.

"I–I know what you're talking about, Danny," she managed at last. "Won't you help me to accept Him as my Savior the way you helped Kirk?"

His heart rejoiced as they prayed together.

She soon looked up, wiping the tears from her smiling face. "This is going to be a wonderful Christmas," she said softly, "the most wonderful Christmas our family has ever had."

***

Tex flew over town about nine o'clock, dipping low so that Danny would be sure to see him, and then headed for the airport. Danny and Kay hurried out to meet him.

By the time they reached the airport on the edge of town, Tex had landed and was sitting impatiently in his plane with the motor idling.

"Hurry up, you two," he called to them, flinging open the door.

Danny crawled into the back seat with the luggage and Kay got in front with Tex.

Tex took a compass reading and headed straight northwest into the mounting wind. He flew low, watching the snow-covered terrain below for landmarks to keep him on his route.

Danny looked at the dark, forbidding clouds and the white-shrouded forest below them. He liked flying in the wintertime too, seeing the clean, white snow with deer and moose standing out in sharp silhouette as they scrounged for food and the unbroken stretches of snow and ice that blanketed the sleeping lakes. But more than ever he liked it because he was going home!

Without closing his eyes, he could see his mom and dad sitting in front of the old barrel-type wood stove. Ron and Roxie would be helping to decorate the Christmas tree or dancing excitedly before the windows watching for the plane.

He thought of the game he had bought for Ron and the doll Kay helped him pick out for Roxie. They weren't much as far as cost was concerned, but he could hardly wait to see their eyes when they opened the packages.

A gust of wind lurched the plane sharply just then and Tex whistled between his teeth. "Say now," he exclaimed, "we can get along without any more of that."

Kay tightened her grip on the edge of the seat, and her face paled as the snow swept past the windshield of the bucking little plane and blotted out the view of the ground below. But she did not speak.

"We're running into a bit of a front," Tex explained evenly. The wind was howling around the little craft, shoving and tearing at it. Danny leaned forward and saw that the air speed was dropping ominously.

"W-where are we, Tex?" he asked.

"We passed Baudette about 20 minutes ago," he said, "and we're out over the Big Traverse. We ought to be over Oak Island any minute now."

"We're not so far from home, Kay," Danny said. "Another 10 minutes and we ought to be there."

At that moment the motor sputtered spasmodically and Tex straightened quickly.

"What was that?" Danny demanded.

While they listened breathlessly, the motor faltered again.

CHAPTER 3

A BAD STORM

The motor caught momentarily with a heartening roar, but the Stinson lurched and shuddered in the sea of snow like an oak leaf tossed by the wind. The storm was howling its fury now, almost blotting out the landing skis and the tips of the wings.

The plane bucked savagely, slamming Kay against the door and sending Danny sprawling over the suitcases. Then, with sickening speed, the storm-tossed craft dropped away. Kay screamed and Danny grabbed for the back of the seat, certain that they were crashing into the trees, or the desolate, frozen lake.

But then, at the last instant, the plane caught and lifted again. Danny sucked in his breath sharply and leaned forward. Tex was calmly working the controls; his lips were set in a thin, hard line and his hand quivered slightly on the wheel.

"A down draft," he said evenly.

The throbbing motor sputtered again and Tex began to work the controls frantically. But this time the little plane nosed slowly downward.

"We're in a tough spot," Tex said. "If you kids have ever prayed you'd better start now."

Danny braced himself and grabbed the seat with both hands. Kay had half turned to face Tex, her lips moving silently. For some reason all the panic had gone from her face and she was smiling a little.

"I'm really not afraid," she told them. "If the Lord wants to take me Home now, it's all right with me."

"O Lord Jesus," Danny prayed to himself. "Just be with us and care for us and help us to get down safely. And, O Lord, just help me to have faith as strong as Kay's."

The motor sputtered and popped as the plane glided uncertainly through the turbulent, snow-filled skies toward the ground.

"If we can just find a hole where we can see a little something," Tex muttered under his breath. "If–" He stopped suddenly. There in the swirling snow before them was a little clump of trees.

"Flag Island!" Danny shouted exuberantly. "Flag Island!"

"We can thank God," Kay replied reverently.

"We're not down yet," Tex warned them.

Just how they managed to get down safely none of them quite knew. The wind was tearing at the frail wings. As the skis touched the ice, a fresh gust hit the plane, sending it careening toward the rock-lined shore. Only Tex's skill at the controls kept them from smashing. Finally, as they came to a stop on the shore of the island, a final fierce blast of wind nosed the plane over.

They sat stiffly in the cabin for a moment or two, as though trying to realize what had happened. Then Tex put his hand on the door handle.

"We'd better get out and get the plane tied down and find shelter somewhere," he said. "There's no telling how long this storm's going to last or how bad it's going to get."

"We're not far from Doc Jenkins' resort, are we?" Danny asked.

"Just over the hill," Tex said. "But there's no one there now. He leaves before cold weather."

"We can get in out of the wind and snow anyway," Danny went on.

They climbed out of the plane, bracing themselves against the icy blast of the wind, and securely tied Tex's plane to the nearest trees. Danny was panting hard by the time they finished, and the snow was stinging his face and neck. Kay was standing with her back hunched against the wind.

"Let's go!" Tex shouted above the storm.

Although they were only a few hundred yards from the resort buildings, it seemed to take hours of plowing through the soft new snow, and they were chilled to the marrow of their bones when they finally stumbled up to the main lodge door and threw it open.

"Whew!" Tex exclaimed, stomping the snow off his boots and rubbing his hands over his frostbitten face. "That was as bad as any storm I ever want to be out in."

Danny started to speak, but a voice from the far corner of the darkened lodge interrupted him.

"Thank God, you've come," a woman's voice said fervently.

"What?" Danny cried. He and Tex and Kay whirled to face the stranger.

There were a man and a woman and two children huddled together under an old bear rug.

"We've been praying and praying for help," the man said slowly, getting to his feet.

"But where did you come from?" Tex asked. "How did you ever get here?"

The family told a strange story that Danny wouldn't have believed had he not known what foolish things some tourists do. Coming into Warroad on a trip from their home in Alabama, they saw fishermen driving their cars on the ice and decided to do likewise.

"We just kept going and going," Mrs. Marshall said, "until the first thing we knew it started to snow something terrible."

"We started back then," her husband continued, "but we got stuck and had an awful time getting over here."

"You were mighty fortunate," Tex replied. "If you'd gotten stuck out on the Big Traverse you'd have all frozen to death."

Mr. and Mrs. Marshall looked at one another and shuddered.

"But then we were lucky too," Tex went on. "If we had been forced down out there the same thing would have happened to us."

"It wasn't luck, Tex," Kay contradicted quietly, "that we were able to find Flag Island."

He was silent for a long while. "I guess you're right at that," he replied.

"Do you think we could get our car out of the snowdrift and – and drive over to this Angle Inlet, or wherever it is?" Mr. Marshall asked.

Tex shook his head. "The drifts will be piled high around the islands."

"But what are we going to do?" Mrs. Marshall cried. "We've got two babies here and we don't have any food for them or anything."

"Hey," Danny exclaimed. "Doesn't old Mr. Moore have a power sled, Tex?"

"That's right." Tex replied, his voice rising excitedly. "I sold him the motor out of my Piper Cub for it about a year ago."

"We're not too far from his shack either," Danny went on. "Maybe you and I could get over there, Tex, and get him to take us to my parents."

Danny and Tex pulled on their boots and went outside hurriedly during a lull in the blinding snowstorm. It was only half a mile to the old bachelor's shack on the other side of the island, but they ran all the way, floundering through the drifts, scrambling over rocks and around fallen trees. At any moment the storm could start up again.

Fortunately, Mr. Moore was home. Without a word he got into his coat and went out to his sled, a half-filled gas can in his hand. In five minutes they had skirted the island and stopped in front of the resort lodge.

"Better get those people out here fast," he mumbled. "This storm's going to start roaring again any time now."

It was a short 20 minutes after Kay and Mrs. Marshall and the two children climbed onto the crude sled and crouched down behind the heavy wooden windbreak that they came roaring up to the Orlis cabins at Angle Inlet.

"Here you be," Moore said as the last one clambered out.

Then, before they had a chance to thank him, he had whirled his clumsy craft about and went roaring back toward his cabin.

Ron and Roxie came dashing to the door.

"It's Danny!" they cried excitedly. "It's Danny and a whole bunch of people!"

CHAPTER 4

TRAPPING

For three days the blizzard raged, piling snow high against the sides of the buildings and blotting out all the familiar landmarks. With the Marshall family and Tex and Kay, in addition to their own family, the Orlis cabin was bulging, but Danny's mom had made beds on the floor and found enough to eat for everyone.

"I just hate to crowd you like this," Mrs. Marshall apologized as the two women and Kay did the dishes.

"Up here we're used to having emergencies," Mrs. Orlis told her. "Besides, we're really thankful that we could have you with us. It makes Christmas more real somehow to have a lot of children around."

"I don't think we'll ever forget this Christmas," Mrs. Marshall went on. "To think that the twins took things of their own and wrapped them for our youngsters so they would get gifts too. And then the way Mr. Orlis read the Bible story of Jesus's birth. It did something to us. I don't think Harold and I will ever be the same again."

"I'm glad if we've helped to make the Lord Jesus more real to you," Danny's mom said.

"We've been Christians for a long while," she continued, "but somehow it didn't mean much how we lived. From now on we're going to live the way Christ would want us to. Things are going to be different in our home."

Kay told Danny about it that afternoon as they sat before the roaring wood stove playing Chinese checkers.

"It's great, isn't it?" he answered.

"It makes us see that God has a plan for us, doesn't it?" she went on.

Kay moved her last marble and won the game. "There," she said triumphantly, "I guess that ought to hold you for a while. Or do you want to get beaten again?"

"I think you're out of my class," he laughed. He got up at that and walked to the window and looked out at the drifting snow. "I've been hoping this storm would let up a little so I could show you something of what our country is like up here, but I'm afraid we're not going to get very far from the fire this vacation."

"As long as it's like this," she said, "it suits me fine. I begin to freeze just to think about what it's doing outside."

Sometime during the night the storm began to ease, and the next morning dawned bright and clear.

"Well," Tex said at breakfast, "it looks like you can get rid of some of your star boarders today, Mrs. Orlis. "I want to go dig my plane out of the snow and get back to Baudette, and I imagine the Marshalls will be wanting to get on their way."

"We'll have to be going just as quickly as we can," Mr. Marshall said. "But what about our car?"

"I'm afraid the best we can do about that is to get it up on Flag Island where we can leave it," Mr. Orlis said. "You'd never be able to get it back to Warroad or Baudette now. It will have to go out with 'Cap' on a barge after the ice goes out in the spring."

Danny and Kay put on snowshoes and made their way over to the neighbor's to borrow his power sled, while Mrs. Marshall helped Danny's mom with the dishes and then packed their suitcases.

The next few days Danny and Ron and Roxie showed Kay the Angle country. They taught her to ski and took her over to the schoolhouse where the twins went, up Harrison Creek to the place where an old cow moose spent the winter, and down to Magnuson's Island to see old Fort Charles, or the place where the old fort used to be.

The weather had been ideal for several days after the storm, but now heavy, sullen gray clouds were beginning to scud across the sky, and the wind gave evidence of rising. Danny stopped for a moment on his skis and listened to the biting wind hit the naked arms of the trees.

"I hope we don't have another storm until after this vacation is over."

The clouds were still moving ominously the next morning and the thermometer had plummeted to 32 below zero. But as soon as their morning devotions were over, Danny began to get ready for the trap line run.

"Do you think you ought to go today?" his mom asked nervously. "It's so terribly cold and the way those clouds look it could start to snow any time."

"I should run my traps, Mom," Ron said. "It's been several days since I've been over them."

"The cold won't bother us," Danny reminded her, "if we put plenty of heavy clothes on. And I can watch the clouds. We can get back in plenty of time if it should start to snow."

"I know you and Ron could," she answered, "but it's Roxie and Kay that I'm thinking of. They aren't used to being out in weather like this."

"Well," Danny said, "Ron and I could hurry over the trap line and get back as soon as we could."

He looked over at Roxie. "We–we want to go along, Danny," she said. "Don't we, Kay?"

"Yes," the girl answered, "but we want to do what your mom thinks is best."

"I'll tell you what, Mom," Danny put in. "The girls can go along as far as the old homesteader's shack. They could stop there while Ron and I go on."

"Well," Mrs. Orlis said uncertainly, "I suppose that would be all right."

Roxie threw her arms about her mom's neck and kissed her impulsively.

Mrs. Orlis fixed a thermos of hot cocoa and some sandwiches, while Danny and Ron got a half-dozen new traps that Tex had brought out on his last trip with the mail.

"I guess we're all set now," Danny called, coming to the kitchen door.

"I'll be ready in a minute," Kay answered. She wriggled into Mrs. Orlis's heavy coat and mittens and pulled a fur cap down over her ears.

"I feel like a polar bear."

They started out on their skis, poling effortlessly along. Although warmly dressed, the frigid air still bit through their clothing and stung the little slits of flesh that were exposed about their eyes.

"A person wouldn't want to stand around long in this," Kay said breathlessly. "Every time I stop I can just feel the cold creep in."

"You're right about that," Danny told her. "When you stop, the cold begins to get you fast. If you're outside here, you've got to keep moving."

Ron's trap line started about a half mile from home and ran along the lake shore to Poplar Creek, where the homesteader's shack still stood. From there one branch went down the creek and the other across the bay toward the old Dawson trail.

Ron found two muskrats and a mink in his first dozen traps. "Hey, this is going to be a good haul," he said, throwing them in the sack he had brought along.

Danny helped him reset the traps while the girls skied on ahead. The wind was rising a little and he noticed that Roxie was beginning to shiver, so he suggested that Kay take her on to the shack. By the time he and Ron reached the cabin he had begun to wish that they had come alone. The snow was beginning to fall silently, and an ominous hush had settled over the Angle. By nightfall the chances were that another blizzard would be lashing the Lake-of-the-Woods country.

"We'd better leave you and Roxie here, Kay," he said as he built a fire in the stove. "I'll take one branch of the trap line and Ron can take the other. That way we can be back here in half the time and get back home before it starts to storm."

"You aren't scared, are you?" Ron asked.

"No," Kay laughed, "we're not afraid to be alone."

"If you could see where Kay and her mom live, Ron," Danny told him, "you wouldn't ask that."

He pulled on his mittens once more. "Do you want to take Laddie with you, Ron," he asked, "or should I take him?"

Ron called to the big collie, but Laddie took a quick look back at him and slunk along beside Danny.

"Well, you come with me, old man," Danny said. "You can be with Ron all winter."

Danny hurried as fast as he could over the snow. It reminded him of the time when he used to spend all winter up on the Angle and worked this same trap line, setting the traps in much the same places for the same kind of fur.

He had stopped at 10 or 15 traps with only a single muskrat to show for his efforts. But it was no wonder. Ron hadn't made the sets right to begin with. Although it took time, he changed four or five of the worst ones before he noticed that the snow was coming down heavier.

"I've got to get going," he muttered to himself. "But I'm going to have to bring Ron out here and teach him how to make some of these water sets."

One more trap and he was going home. Ron had set it about 50 feet off shore in a place that didn't look too likely. Danny broke the new ice out of the hole with his ax and, in his hurry, reached down with his hand to see whether there was anything in the trap. Ron had set the trap too close to the surface, right under the ice. As Danny cautiously inched his mittened fingers downward, he touched the trigger. The vicious steel jaws snapped shut on his hand.

CHAPTER 5

HELP! HELP!

Sharp, blinding pain swept over Danny as he lay there with his arm outstretched, his fingers imprisoned in the steel jaws of the trap beneath the ice. How could it possibly have happened! He had been sliding his mittened hand carefully into the icy water to find the trap chain, for he wanted only to check the trap to see whether Ron had caught a beaver or not. But without warning, the trap had sprung at him. He was trapped! Trapped! Sweat broke out on his forehead and for a brief instant his head reeled.

Gritting his teeth Danny pulled savagely on his hand! Sharp, throbbing pains surged up into his shoulder! Ron's traps were new, and the steel teeth bit even deeper through the heavy leather mitten into his fingers as he pulled. For once the set had been properly made, the trap anchored securely under the ice. An odd, sickening feeling welled up in his stomach. He collapsed, panting, on the ice.

Laddie, sensing that something was wrong, edged closer to him licking at his face.

"Don't, old man!" he gasped. "Stop it, Laddie!" The dog dropped beside him and whimpered softly.

It was beginning to snow harder now. Pellets as hard as sand stung Danny's face and sent a chill through his heavy clothing. By this time the icy water had penetrated his mitten and sleeve and threatened to freeze his arm. He had to free himself. He had to!

His ax! If only he could reach his ax! He had laid it aside so carelessly a moment or two before. If he could get to it there was a chance he could chop the hole big enough to get the trap up on top of the ice! Or he might be able to get his other hand down to where he could loosen the spring. It was only a chance!

Biting his lips to force down the pain, he began to scoot his body, an inch at a time, toward the handle. His fingers groped desperately. He was close enough to touch it with the tip of his leather mitten. Another inch! Another fraction of an inch!

"O Lord Jesus," he prayed, "help me to get the ax. Just–" But even as he prayed, he hit the handle in his desperation and knocked it further away. He groaned inwardly. He could never get it now.

His heart pounding furiously he cried, "Laddie, fetch! Fetch!"

Ordinarily his dog would go get anything he wanted him to. But this time he couldn't seem to understand. The big dog took four or five steps away from Danny, then stopped uncertainly and came back.

"Fetch, Laddie!" he cried again. "Fetch!"

Danny's arm was numb, save for the creeping cold that had already driven to the very depths of his body. Cold sweat froze against the rim of his fur-trimmed cap and his legs began to twitch.

It would be hours until somebody found him. By then it would be too late!

Danny Orlis raised his head a little and looked around. The trap that had caught him was the last one on the line. Just around the next finger of land stood the shack where Kay and Roxie were waiting.

"Help!" he shouted into the teeth of the rising wind. If only he could make them hear him!

Laddie took up the cry, barking furiously. But it was no use. Who could hear a dog and a boy in the face of a wind like that? Danny dropped, exhausted, to the snow.

Back in the homesteader's cabin, Ron walked nervously to the window and looked out.

"I can't understand what's happened to Danny," he said. "I've made that circle lots of times and it never did take me this long."

"Maybe he got lost," Roxie ventured.

"He wouldn't get lost over there," Ron said. "The line doesn't even go into the woods. Anybody could run it without getting lost. Something must have happened to him."

Roxie's eyes widened. "What are we going to do?" she trembled. "What are we going to do?"

"It doesn't do any good to go to pieces," Kay told them. "We ought to pray for Danny and – and then go out to look for him."

"But it's snowing harder than ever," the younger girl protested. "We'll never find him."

While they knelt in prayer, Kay heard the faint barking of a dog. They heard it again, just as they finished.

"What was that?" Kay asked suddenly. "What was that?"

"I didn't hear anything," Ron replied.

"I did," she retorted. "It sounded like–"

"It's Laddie!" Roxie exclaimed.

"Are you sure?"

"It's Laddie, all right!" Ron said. "I'd know that bark anywhere. Danny must be coming!"

"Isn't it wonderful how quickly God answers prayer?" Roxie asked. "Here we just prayed that Danny would get here safely. Now he's coming."

But minutes passed and there was no sign of him. They went to the door of the shack and looked out. There was nothing in view except fresh, drifting snow.

"Are we sure we heard a dog?" Kay asked uncertainly. "Perhaps we just imagined it."

The twins nodded solemnly. "That was Laddie, all right."

As though to prove them right, the sharp staccato bark sounded again.

Kay picked up her coat.

"Where are you going in this storm?" Roxie asked.

"Danny must be hurt," she said determinedly. "I'm going out there."

"I'm going with you," Ron informed her.

"I'm going too," added Roxie.

The three of them put on their skis and started off slowly through the drifting snow toward the place where they had heard the barking.

"It's got to be on the trap line," Ron said. "That much is certain."

They started around the line the same way Danny had gone, but Laddie soon barked again, and Ron stopped.

"That came from over there." He pointed toward the west.

Kay took the lead this time, shoving over the snow as fast as she dared without running away from Roxie.

She saw Laddie first, a dim, formless shape hunched in the snow! There was Danny, stretched out on the ice! The new fall of snow had already covered his ankles and the calves of his legs. Her heart began to hammer a frantic beat against her sheep-lined coat, and her arms were trembling.

"There he is!" she cried, driving forward on her skis. "O Lord Jesus!" she prayed inwardly. "Don't let him be badly hurt! Please don't let him be hurt!"

"Are you all right, Danny?" she asked, kneeling beside him. "Are you all right?"

He was breathing heavily and his eyes were open.

"Got caught in my own trap," he managed.

Ron helped Kay get the older boy's hand out of the powerful beaver trap. The instant he pulled his dripping arm out of the water it was encased in ice.

"Are you all right, Danny?" Kay asked once more.

"I–I think so," he stammered, his teeth chattering. "I–I think I'm all right."

He moved a stride or two forward, uncertainly. Then his knees began to sag. Kay and Ron caught him.

"Come on, Ron," Kay said evenly. "We've got to get him back to the shack."

She looked down at his injured hand, gasping when she saw that the torn mitten was soaked with blood.

Once inside the little cabin, Kay and Ron helped Danny out of his coat and jacket and made him lie down on the rough pine boards before the stove.

"Is he going to be all right?" Roxie asked anxiously. "Is he, Kay?"

"We'll have to trust the Lord Jesus to help Danny get all right," she answered, tenderly.

Kay had the faith to believe what she was saying, but when she looked at Danny her heart sank. Blood was oozing from his torn fingers, and his lips were blue with cold. He had been lying very still on the floor. Now he began to shake violently.

"What's wrong?" Roxie demanded. "What's happening to him?"

"Get your coat and put it over him, Roxie," Kay said, spreading her own heavy coat over the injured boy. "He's in shock right now. We've got to keep him warm."

She knew about shock. She had been with her mom often enough on accident calls in Mexico to have seen what it could do.

"You–you'd better get some more wood, Ron," she said, trying to keep the fear out of her voice, "if you can get it without going too far away."

"Sure thing." Ron got to his feet and picked up his ax. He and the dog went hurriedly outside.

Roxie went over to where Kay was sitting and slid in under her arm. "I–I'm scared, Kay," she whispered. "I–I'm awfully scared."

Kay bit her lip sharply, and for a heartbeat or two she found it impossible to speak. But when she did, her voice was calm and clear.

"We have Christ to watch over us, darling," she said softly. "We've committed Danny to His care. He'll work things out according to His plan."

Roxie smiled weakly and winked back the tears.

When Ron came back into the cabin, his arms loaded with wood, Kay went over to him and said softly, "Do you think you and Laddie could make it home?"

He looked up quickly. "Why?"

She glanced toward the injured boy. His face was already flushed with fever.

"We've got to get help for Danny," Kay whispered, "as quickly as we can!"

CHAPTER 6

RESCUED!

Ron looked toward Danny who was lying so still on the rough pine floor.

"You'd better hurry," Kay said, trying to sound firm and unafraid.

Ron picked up his heavy mittens. "Do you think he's going to be all right, Kay?" he asked tensely.

"Of course he is!"

Ron moved hesitantly toward the door, Laddie at his side. Then he stopped and turned back. "I can't leave you and Roxie alone here with him!" he blurted.

"You've got to, Ron," Kay told him sternly. "That's the only possible way we can get help!"

Danny opened his eyes for a moment. Gritting his teeth to force back the blinding pain, he raised up on one elbow.

"Kay's right," he said softly. "You go and get Dad, Ron. I'll be all right." He bit his lip savagely as a wave of nausea gripped him.

Kay followed Ron outside. "Whatever you do," she cautioned, "hurry!"

He nodded grimly.

Kay watched him a moment, unmindful of the stinging cold on her face and arms. He had to get through safely – and soon. He had to!

With a prayer in her heart, she turned and went back into the little one-room cabin. She was still shivering with cold when she knelt beside the sick boy. He was conscious, but his eyes were closed and he was breathing heavily. His forehead was burning and dry to the touch. His pulse was racing.

"O Lord Jesus!" she prayed silently. "Help me to do the right things to take care of Danny. And send help here in time!"

She was still praying when Roxie leaned over her, her little face pinched and drawn and her small fingers trembling on Kay's shoulder.

"I–I'm scared," the younger girl said hoarsely. "I'm awfully scared."

Kay drew the frightened girl down beside her. "We shouldn't be frightened, dear," she said. "You know the Lord watches over us and takes care of us, don't you?"

She nodded solemnly, winking back the tears.

"If we pray and ask Him to help us He will," she went on.

"I know," Roxie replied uncertainly, "but Danny's so awfully sick, a–and his hand is hurt so bad! And– and he's the only big brother I've got."

"It's times like these when we have to put our trust in God," the older girl said. "Did Danny ever tell you how God took care of us down in Mexico last summer?"

She nodded again, swallowing hard.

"He'll do the same way for us now," Kay continued. "He's the same God – the same God who helped the disciples even. If we put our trust in Him, He'll help us."

Roxie quieted somewhat. "Did you pray," she asked, "when those guys down in Mexico were after you?"

"Of course we did," Kay answered. "We were praying all the time. We hurried as fast as we could, too, but we certainly prayed."

"Would you help me to pray now?" Roxie asked. "The way you and Danny and Jim did last summer?"

Together they knelt beside the roaring wood stove and talked to God about Danny and Ron.

"And Lord Jesus," she prayed earnestly, "if it gets dark before they get back, please light the way for them."

They got to their feet. Roxie took Kay's hand and squeezed it hard. "I'm not afraid anymore."

The older girl looked down at her and smiled. "Neither am I," she replied.

Together they sat down beside the stove. Roxie leaned back in Kay's arm and closed her eyes. For the moment at least, Danny was resting more comfortably. His breathing was more natural and he didn't twitch and turn as he had before.

For half an hour or more Kay sat there while Danny's sister drifted off into troubled sleep. The girl tossed fitfully and mumbled something, half aloud. The fire died to embers and a chill began to creep through the cabin walls. Kay withdrew her arm as carefully as she could and laid Roxie's head on the floor. She got to her feet then and rebuilt the fire in the stove with the birch bark and pine boughs Ron had brought in.

Danny stirred restlessly, and the coats he was covered with fell back from his shoulders. Kay knelt beside him and pulled them up, brushing his cheek with her hand. He was resting more easily but his fever was mounting. That much was certain. Why didn't they come? Why didn't they come?

She didn't have a watch and dared not risk waking Danny, but it had been dark outside for a long while. The merry, crackling fire sent dancing slivers of light about the little cabin, but shadows hid the corners and gave vague, unfamiliar shapes to the few crude pieces of furniture inside.

Kay got up and walked to the frost-covered window and peered intently outside, listening for Ron and Mr. Orlis. But there was no sound. It seemed as though the rest of the world had been swallowed up, leaving them alone in the bleak little cabin.

Roxie half awakened and sat up, whimpering. Kay went back to her quickly, cradling her head in her arm and talking softly to her. Soon she went to sleep again.

And so did Kay.

She didn't mean to. She fought against it, trying to stay awake in case Danny or Roxie needed her. But it had grown so warm in the cabin. Her eyelids had become as heavy as her aching heart. She closed her eyes and dropped off to sleep.

How long she slept she didn't know, but she was awakened suddenly by the sound of heavy footsteps and loud, excited voices.

"Say, now," Mr. Orlis called, his big voice booming through the cabin, "what's going on here?"

Danny and Kay awakened instantly.

Mr. Orlis knelt beside his son, felt his hot forehead and frowned, and took a quick look at his mangled fingers.

"This was a fine trick you pulled, Danny," he said, trying to joke a little. "Getting your fist in your own trap. If you're going to keep up that sort of stuff, don't tell anyone I taught you to trap."

"I know it was a dumb trick," Danny grinned feebly.

Neither Kay nor Danny had noticed that Mrs. Williams, the only trained nurse on the Angle, was there until she knelt beside the injured boy.

"Perhaps you'd better let me take a look at him," she said quietly.

They watched tensely while the nurse took Danny's pulse and temperature and examined his mangled fingers.

"Our big problem here," she said at last, "is exposure and fighting off pneumonia. His hand looks terrible, but it can be fixed up all right." She gave him a big shot of penicillin from the supply which the doctor in Warroad had given her for just such an emergency and got to her feet. "I hate to see you take him out of here, Carl," she said. "He shouldn't be moved." She looked about the drafty, ramshackle little cabin, "But we don't have any choice."

They wrapped Danny in five or six heavy woolen blankets and took him out to the horse-drawn sleigh.

"I'm so glad you got through as quickly as you did, Ron," Kay said softly, as she and the twins huddled together in the big sleigh.

"We prayed for you," his sister informed him.

"Maybe you think I wasn't praying!" Ron replied. "I never stopped skiing or praying all the time I was going."

Kay put her arms about the twins and hugged them both.

Danny Orlis was terribly sick all that night and the next. Mrs. Williams went home with them and slept on a cot beside his bed. Once or twice Kay heard her say that if the fever didn't break soon they'd have to get a doctor up there or get Danny down to the hospital.

But about daylight the second morning his fever broke and he started to get better. Kay could see it without being told as she peeked into his room on her way to breakfast.

"Hi," he grinned at her.

"Hey, you look as though you feel a little better than you did a couple of days ago," she said.

"Yep," he told her. "I'm about ready to stick my other paw in another beaver trap."

"If you do," she said, "do it when I'm not around."

In a few minutes, his dad came in with a letter.

"This came yesterday, Danny," he said. "But I didn't think you felt up to looking at it until this morning."

Danny glanced at the envelope. "It's from Coach Masters. I wonder what he wants."

He tore open the envelope and read the short letter. The smile left his face.

"What's the matter?" Kay asked him.

"Coach Masters wrote," he said slowly. "He wants me to play hockey. Maybe with the varsity."

"That's wonderful, Danny!" Kay cried. "That's what we've been praying about. Now maybe you'll have a chance to win Rick and some of the other guys to Christ."

He shook his head miserably. "Maybe I could have," he said, "but look at this." He held up his mangled hand.

CHAPTER 7

BACK AT SCHOOL

Danny Orlis got up for a short time that afternoon. Wrapped in a heavy woolen blanket, he sat in a chair before the big wood stove. Mrs. Williams had checked his temperature just before dinner. When she found it was normal she gave him another shot of penicillin, cautioned him to stay inside for two or three days, and hurried up frozen Angle Bay to her own family.

Danny stretched out in the chair and closed his eyes. It was good to be up again. For the moment he forgot his injured hand and the letter from the hockey coach at Cedarton.

The weather had warmed a little. Ron and Mr. Orlis were out getting wood. Kay and his mom were in the kitchen doing the dinner dishes. And he was alone in the living room.

Danny straightened and looked at his watch. The team would be in their uniforms about now and lacing up their skates. A lump of ice formed in the pit of his stomach. He took Coach Masters' letter from his pocket and read it for the sixth time.

"Dear Danny," the hockey coach had written. "I wanted to get an opportunity to talk with you before you left town, but I checked your boarding house after you had already gone. I'm convinced that you were sincere in your reason for not playing football last fall. I want you on the hockey team. In fact, we need you desperately–"

Danny stopped reading and held up his injured fingers. How could he play hockey with a hand like that? Slowly he tried to bend his swollen fingers. Fierce barbs of pain stabbed up his arm. Cold beads of sweat moistened his forehead. He bit his lower lip and gulped hard.

When Kay came in he was staring blankly at the floor.

"What's the matter, Danny?" she asked. "Is your hand still bothering?"

"It isn't that," he told her. "I just want to play hockey, that's all. And I won't be able to do it. I couldn't even bend my fingers to get them around a stick."

"Does it mean that much to you, Danny?" she asked.

He grinned crookedly. "It's not only playing hockey," he said. "I've been thinking about Rick Haines and Butch and Eddie Chambers and all the rest. This would have given me a chance to witness to them."

The next three or four days crept slowly past. School had already started after the Christmas vacation.

Kay and Danny were both anxious to get back to Cedarton, but they had to wait until Mrs. Williams thought Danny was well enough to travel.

Finally, however, he was permitted to go. Tex flew up after them and took them down to the little Minnesota community where they were going to school.

"It's going to be good to get back to school," Kay said excitedly as they walked over the crisp, hard-packed snow from the airport to town. "I hope we don't have too much work to make up."

"Yeh," Danny replied woodenly.

"You don't act very enthused about it," she told him. "You sound the way Ron did when I asked him if he liked his teacher."

"I've been wondering something," he said, more to himself than to Kay.

"Now what?" she asked.

"Maybe I could hold a hockey stick with one hand!"

"Danny Orlis!" she exclaimed horrified. "You aren't foolish enough to try to play hockey when you've got a hand like that, are you?"

"I might be able to get by in practice," he said seriously, "well enough to learn the plays, so I could get into a few games when my hand does get all right."

When Danny got to the Barber house, Kirk and Guy Allen were lying on their stomachs listening to a Bible story program. They didn't even hear him come in and walk past them on the way to his room.

Later that evening when Mrs. Barber called the family in to supper, Danny turned to Kirk. "Hey," he said, "it's good to see Guy Allen here."

"He's my friend."

Danny saw then that Mrs. Barber's face was glowing in a way that he had never seen it before. She looked younger somehow and more relaxed, as though she wasn't worrying the way she used to.

"You know, Danny," she said when she saw that he was looking at her, "I've been a different woman since I accepted the Lord Jesus. I used to worry about everything, and Christmas and days like that would be terrible for me. But this Christmas was marvelous. I don't know how anyone can even think they can get along without the Lord."

The next afternoon after school, Danny went out for hockey with the rest of the guys. Coach Masters saw his hand and tried to persuade him against it.

"You couldn't even hold a stick."

"I think I could," Danny said. "I've played one-handed quite a little."

"Well," the coach said reluctantly, "we're going to have a light scrimmage tonight. I'll let you try it, Danny, but I'm not in favor of it."

Danny went over beside Rick and sat down on the bench to unlace his shoes.

"What're you doing here?" Rick asked sullenly. "I thought we didn't want you playing hockey with us."

"I thought maybe you had changed your mind," Danny said, trying to laugh.

Rick Haines stared at him, then got up significantly and moved. As he did so, the guy who sat down on the other side of Danny moved too, leaving him alone.

Danny got into his uniform and skates and made his way out onto the ice. It didn't make any difference whether he could play with an injured hand or not. He wasn't going to be able to make friends with the guys.

He stopped before the rack and selected a small light stick and skated out onto the ice. He skated slowly around the rink to get the feel of the ice and to limber his legs. Then he called for a puck and darted at top speed from one goal to the other, dribbling it expertly. It wasn't as natural using one hand on the stick, but he could manage. He knew that now.

Rick Haines, who had been standing on the sidelines talking with two or three girls, left them suddenly as Danny approached and snaked out toward him, his stick outstretched.

Danny saw him from the corner of one eye. He knew what Rick was doing. Without seeming to, he skated slower until the other hockey player was almost on him. Then in one lightning movement he faked so cleverly that Rick sprawled headlong across the ice. A chorus of laughter went up from the spectators.

The other boy scrambled to his feet and took after Danny, his skates knifing over the ice and his stick flailing. He may have been after the puck, but it didn't appear that way. He was skating too hard and fast and was coming up on Danny from behind at an angle that wouldn't possibly let him reach the hard rubber puck. Somebody yelled a warning and Danny started to turn. But he was not fast enough. Rick hit him squarely, sending him sprawling.

His mangled left hand hit the ice. Sharp, sickening pains shot up into his shoulder. His head spun! Cold sweat broke out on his forehead as he tried to turn over. Coach Masters skated out to him.

"Are you all right, Danny?"

"I–I think so," he said.

The coach knelt beside him and helped pull the heavy glove off his throbbing hand. "I don't think any bones are broken," he said, examining them carefully, "but we should have an X-ray to be sure. Get dressed, I'll take you down to the hospital." He turned to Rick. "You, Haines," he said coldly, "go turn in your uniform. You're through for the season!"

"But coach!" he protested.

"You heard me," the coach said. "I let you guys vote Orlis off the team once. Tonight you deliberately skated into him when you knew he was playing with an injured hand. There isn't room enough on the Cedarton team for you." With that he turned sharply and skated after Danny.

Danny wanted to say something, to talk to the coach about Rick, but he didn't dare. Coach Masters' eyes were flashing, and his lips were drawn into a thin, hard line.

The technician X-rayed Danny's hand and the doctor came in and told them there weren't any broken bones.

"But tell me, coach," the doctor said, "is this guy one of your regulars?"

"He will be when we get this hand in shape," the coach told him.

"Why don't you let me make an aluminum guard for that hand?" the doctor went on. "Then this won't happen again."

After the doctor took measurements of Danny's hand, the coach drove him over to Mrs. Barber's and let him off. Kirk met him at the door.

"There's somebody up in your room to see you, Danny."

"Who is it?"

"Rick Haines," Kirk whispered, "and he must be mad or something! I never saw anyone look like he does!"

CHAPTER 8

THE APOLOGY

Danny looked first at Kirk and then up the stairway toward his room. Rick Haines was the last person he had expected to come and see him. Especially after what had happened at hockey practice an hour or so before.

"What did he say he wanted?" Danny asked.

"He didn't say," Kirk replied, "but he sure acted funny. His face was awful white and his voice trembled when he talked. He–he sort of scared me."

"I'll see what he's got on his mind," Danny said evenly.

He walked unhesitatingly up the steps and into his room. Rick Haines was sitting on the chair at his desk. His face was pale and drawn. His hands were clenched so tightly that the veins stood out.

"Hi, Rick!" Danny said, closing the door. "Kirk told me you were here and I came right up." He took off his cap and coat. "Sure is cold, isn't it?"

Rick stared at him without answering.

Danny pulled up a chair and sat down. "What's on your mind?" he asked.

Rick started to speak, then stopped. He chewed on his lip nervously.

Danny waited, half expecting his tall guest to pounce on him at any moment.

"I want to talk to you about what happened tonight," Rick blurted at last.

"I was sorry about what the coach did, Rick. I didn't want him to kick you off the team."

"I'm the one who ought to apologize," the other boy said. "I got what I deserved. I got mad when you faked the puck away from me. I ran into you on purpose. I should've been kicked off the team. That–that's what I came over here to tell you."

"You don't have to apologize. It's all right with me."

That tense, strained look was still on Rick's face.

"I'll go to the coach tomorrow," Danny said.

"That isn't bothering me," Rick replied, "but there's something else that is."

Danny leaned forward expectantly.

"I–I don't know where to begin, Danny. I used to go to Sunday school and church real regular. A couple of times I almost trusted Christ as my Savior. But then I got to running around with some guys that made fun of things like that, and my parents didn't much care one way or another. I finally quit going altogether."

"I see."

"I think that's why I hated you," Rick said. "You had done what I knew I ought to."

"But you can still have it," Danny told him softly. "All you have to do is confess that you are a sinner and put your trust in Jesus. It's as simple as that."

"That's what I came to see you about," the other boy replied tensely. "I saw this afternoon that I'm on the wrong track. I can't go on any longer, Danny. I've got to become a Christian."

Praying for the right words, Danny got his Bible from beside his bed. Carefully he read a few verses that explained the plan of salvation. He read in Isaiah that all men are evil and need a Savior and in John that God sent Christ to save those who are lost.

Rick slid out onto the edge of the chair, clasping and relaxing his hands nervously.

Finally, Danny Orlis looked up. "You do believe that you are a sinner, don't you?" he asked.

Rick nodded, pressing his lips together tightly.

"You know that sinners have earned death, don't you?" he persisted. "That you really deserve to be lost because of the sin in your life?"

"That's why I came here tonight."

"Then you do believe that Christ has the power to save," Danny continued, "and that if you confess your sins and put your trust in Him you will be saved?"

Rick Haines nodded again. "I do, Danny," he said earnestly, "and I'm ready to put my trust in Him."

"You've got to mean business with God," Danny said, choosing his words prayerfully. "It wouldn't do any good for you to go through the motions of accepting Christ as your Savior if you don't mean business. You'll have to quit doing those things you know are wrong and try your best to live as Jesus would have you to live."

"I'm ready to do that, Danny."

Together they got down on their knees and prayed. Rick's prayer was simple, but very much in earnest. It was easy for Danny to tell that every word came from the depths of his heart. When they got to their feet at last, Rick grinned crookedly.

"Hey, this has taken a load off me," he said fervently.

"You'll never know how happy it has made me," Danny said. "I've been praying and praying for you."

Rick Haines would have gone with Danny and Kay to Pastor Carlstrom's home that evening to make plans for the new Bible Club, but he had to study for a test in American History the next morning. Danny could scarcely wait to tell Kay what had happened.

"I've got some news for you," he said as they walked toward the pastor's home together.

"What's that?" she asked.

"Another charter member for the Bible Club," he answered casually.

"Kirk?"

"Someone older than he."

Kay was thrilled as Danny told her what had happened.

"I guess you were right," she said. "The Lord did use hockey to help you witness to the guys."

"It didn't happen quite like I thought it would, but it worked out."

Pastor Carlstrom was as excited as they were about Rick becoming a Christian. "It shows how much we need a Bible Club," he said. "It will help to get Richard grounded in the Scriptures. That's what he's got to have."

They discussed several men who might serve as an adult sponsor and decided on the evening they would first try to get the group together. Before they realized it, the clock struck 9:30.

"I've got to be going," Danny said, getting to his feet. "We've got a hockey game in a couple of nights and I've got to be in by 10:00."

The next morning he went to school early and talked with Coach Masters about Rick.

"I appreciate your coming, Danny," he said, "but we can't tolerate violent behavior."

"I'm sure it won't happen again."

"I'll talk to you about it again after the game Friday night," the coach said.

Rick was out of school with a bad cold that day and the next. Danny didn't get to talk to him before the first hockey game of the season. But Rick was in the stands. Danny spied him as he skated onto the ice.

"Now, Danny," the coach said, calling him off to one side, "I'm going to use you at wing tonight.

This is only a warmup game and we don't want you to take any chances of getting your hand hurt again. So take it easy."

"Okay."

But his hand didn't bother him during the game. The Crayville squad had only one letterman back and were so inexperienced they scarcely made it a contest. Danny played most of the first half. He started at wing and got along fairly well, but the coach moved him back to defense after he made three goals in twice that many minutes.

At half time, as the team skated off the floor, Mr. Cartwright, Danny's former employer, called. "You've got a sweet-looking wing in Orlis, Masters. But don't count on him too much. He's liable to get religion again like he did during the football season."

Danny's ears reddened as he went into the locker room.

"I've been doing a lot of thinking about Rick," the coach said to Danny. "If he'll come before the squad and apologize to you and to me, I'll let him come back."

Danny told Rick about it, and when the game was over the boy followed the team into the dressing room. The coach quieted the guys.

"I want to apologize to Coach Masters and Danny for what I did the other night," Rick Haines began. "I shouldn't have done it. I'm sorry."

A moment of awkward silence followed.

"But I'm glad that it happened," he went on. "It made me realize that I've been on the wrong road all my life. I talked to Danny and accepted Christ as my Savior. With God's help, I'm going to live as He would have me to live from now on."

The guys stared at him blankly, as though they couldn't believe that it was Rick Haines who was talking.

CHAPTER 9

A NEW WITNESS

The hockey team stood respectfully while Rick told them what the Lord Jesus meant to him. Butch Winston coughed nervously and shifted from one foot to the other. Eddie Chambers, Rick's closest friend, looked quickly away, embarrassed at what he was saying. "I wish I could make all of you guys see how great it is to put your trust in Jesus," he said fervently. "You'll never be sorry if you do."

In the long, uneasy silence that followed, Coach Masters stepped out and looped his arm over Rick's shoulder. "I want you to know," the coach said softly, "that we're all for you. I wish the whole team had what you've got." He stopped for an instant. "The fact is, you make me wish I could have it for myself too."

The boys dressed quietly, and Danny and Rick walked home together.

"I was really proud of you," Danny said as they left the building. "It means something when a Christian's got nerve enough to let his friends know that he loves the Lord. Your testimony got hold of some of the guys tonight."

"I didn't do much," Rick replied. "To tell you the truth I was scared to death." As he talked, he had been going through his pockets carefully. At last he took a package of cigarettes out of his jacket and looked at it significantly. "I haven't worn this coat since I became a Christian," he apologized. With that he broke the cigarettes in two and threw them into the snow. "I guess I'm finished with those."

They walked down to the shop where so many of the guys and girls hung out, waited for a booth, and ordered ice cream.

"I'm so thankful that we've got you to help us with the new Bible Club," Danny said while they were waiting. "Our problem right now is to get the club organized so we can draw the others in."

"You can count on me. I don't know much about the Bible, but I'll do what I can."

"How about Marilyn?" Danny asked. "She'll come along too, won't she?"

"I'm not so sure about her. She's great and all that, but she likes having a good time. The Bible Club will seem like dull stuff to her."

"It isn't going to be dull," Danny assured him. "You wouldn't call Kay dull, would you?"

"There aren't many girls like Kay, though," Rick retorted.

Kay and Danny worked hard Saturday afternoon and evening, talking with kids on the street and calling on them in their homes to interest them in the Bible Club. Most of them didn't seem interested at all. But when they had called at the last home, there were 18 who had definitely promised to come.

"I'm a little disappointed," Danny said. "After the way Rick gave his testimony and all, I thought we'd get most of the hockey squad and a lot of the other kids."

"We've got a good start," Kay told him. "We can't be discouraged about this. If it was easy to get kids interested in spiritual things, the churches would have won them all a long time ago."

"I guess that's right."

"We've got to be just like the missionaries are," she went on. "We've got to introduce the Lord Jesus to those who don't know anything about Him and don't think they want to know Him. This is a wonderful beginning."

"Maybe I want to see too much happen too fast."

They had the first meeting of the Bible Club in Rick Haines' home on Monday night. Kay walked over there with Marilyn. Danny hurried to Rick's to help greet people as they came in. Quite a number of kids outside the church had promised they would be there, but, even with the Christians, there were only

14 or 15. They filed into the big living room and sat down on the overstuffed furniture or on the floor and waited uneasily.

Rick introduced Les Harms, a jovial, gray-haired businessman who had agreed to act as adult sponsor. He had them sing a few choruses with Kay at the piano. As they sang, the tenseness seemed to leave the group. By the time Les began to speak they were sitting comfortably, listening. He gave a short message from the Book of John, there were two or three short prayers, and within the allotted hour it was over.

"Hey," one guy said to his friend as they walked past Danny, "I thought this was going to be dull. I didn't know the Bible could be so interesting. Believe me, I'm coming back next week."

Danny was thrilled as he heard that.

When everyone had gone, except Kay and Marilyn and Danny, they went into the kitchen and raided the refrigerator.

"How do you think it went over?" Rick asked anxiously.

"Great," Danny and Kay chorused.

"Les is going to be a good teacher," the new Christian went on. "The kids all liked him. And believe me, he knows his Bible for a man who isn't a preacher or anything."

"What did you think of it, Marilyn?" Kay asked, turning to the pretty, dark-haired girl.

Color tinged Marilyn's cheeks. She did not answer.

"What did you think of it, Marilyn?" Rick asked, smiling. "You haven't said a word."

She looked down to avoid his steady gaze. "It was all right, I guess."

"All right?" he echoed. "Is that all you've got to say?"

She was silent for a moment. "Well, to tell you the truth," she replied, "I never could agree with him. He said that everybody is a sinner and in need of a Savior. And I–I haven't been so wicked. Why if I had believed everything he said, I'd have felt like the worst sinner in the world."

"That's just the way I felt before I became a Christian," Rick put in earnestly.

"The Bible tells us that we all are sinners," Kay said, "and that the wages of sin is death. That's why we have to confess our sins and put our trust in Jesus to save us."

"I'm all right," Marilyn defended stoutly, "just the way I am. I don't need a Savior."

Rick looked over at Danny appealingly. That young man started to answer her, to tell her more of what the Word of God had to say about sin. But with the words on his lips he stopped. She was angry and wanted only to argue. It wouldn't do any good to keep talking to her now.

"You know, Marilyn," he said instead, "it doesn't make any difference what Rick or Kay or I think about this. Or even what Les Harms thinks. The important thing is, What does the Bible say? Why don't you take your Bible and read the Book of John? See what God says about it. After all, He's the One who does the saving."

"The minister in *our* church doesn't preach about anything like that," she retorted.

Kay looked at her watch and got abruptly to her feet. "It's almost 10:00," she said, "I've got to leave."

As she and Danny walked toward the place where she stayed, he said, "I don't think Marilyn is going to be very good for Rick."

"I was thinking the same thing. We mustn't forget to pray for them."

At hockey practice the next few days, Coach Masters used Danny during the long instruction period when he began to teach the team a new series of plays. But during scrimmage he benched him.

"We're not going to take any chances of hurting that hand."

The few days of rest did begin to make a tremendous difference in Danny's hand. The angry swelling went down, and the fingers began to itch fiercely. "A good sign that they are beginning to heal," Mrs. Barber assured him.

"Another week and you'll be as good as new," the coach said. "Then with you and Rick on the wings we'll go to town."

The fact that Rick had accepted Christ made it easier for Danny. The tall, lanky Haines had the respect and admiration of all the guys in school. For

Danny to be seen with him helped a lot. Yet they had difficulty in getting more than a small handful out for Bible Club.

"I never heard so many excuses in my life," Rick laughed, when a group of guys began to explain why they wouldn't come.

"We'd like to come, Rick," Butch Winston said. "Honest we would. Only–"

"Only what?"

"Only–only–"

"If you can't think of anything better than that, Butch," Haines said good-naturedly, "we'll be expecting you out tomorrow night. And we won't be taking any excuses."

"Okay," Butch said reluctantly. "I guess maybe I can make it."

"Do you think they'll come?" Danny asked when the two of them were alone again.

"They'd better," Rick said. "I'm not going to let up on them until they do. But it isn't the guys I'm worried about, Danny. I can handle them all right. It's Marilyn."

Danny said nothing.

"I've been trying my best to talk to her, but I can't get any place," he continued. "She just won't listen to me. Thinks it's foolish for us to be so concerned about confessing sin and trusting Christ as our Savior. Her dad told her that all of us are brothers and the children of God."

"That isn't what the Bible says."

"I know," Rick said, "but try to tell that to Marilyn."

The next night Rick went to see Marilyn to talk to her about the Bible Club.

"I don't think I'm interested," she said loftily.

"But all our friends will be there."

"I want to see the show that's on that night."

"This is going to be better than any show," Rick said.

For an instant she was silent. Then a little smile lifted one corner of her mouth. "I'll tell you what I'll do, Rick," she offered. "You go to the movie with me on Sunday night and I'll go to Bible Club with you on Monday night."

"But–" he started to protest.

"That's the only way I'll go," she told him flatly.

CHAPTER 10

AN EXCITING GAME

"Well," Rick said hesitantly, "I guess I could, but I'm sort of in a spot. I half promised Danny that I'd go to church with him Sunday night. I hate to back out on my word – especially now."

Marilyn looked at him strangely, then shrugged her shoulders. "Well, suit yourself. But if you want me to go to Bible Club Monday night, you'll have to go to the movie with me on Sunday. I've just got to see that movie. It's a musical and they say it's amazing!"

Rick saw Danny Orlis the next morning on the way to school. He had planned to tell him then, but they got to talking hockey. And when he finally remembered, they were in the schoolhouse and the warning bell had rung. There wasn't any time to talk to Danny before hockey practice either. Half the guys were still lacing their skates when Coach Masters came storming in.

"I was going to see if Miss Johnson would loan me some of her Physical Education Class," he snapped. "I think they could play hockey better than you guys did in last night's scrimmage."

A couple of guys laughed nervously. The coach whirled on them. "This might be funny if it wasn't so serious," he roared.

"Now I want you to get out on that ice and show us some snap. Or we'll be laughed right out of the league."

With that he sent them through a blistering two-hour session on fundamentals.

"Man!" Rick said when they finally finished. "I'm so tired I can hardly take my skates off."

Danny grinned at him. "We skate all day long up at the Angle lots of times," he said.

Just then Mr. Masters stuck his head in the locker room. "We had a rough practice, guys," he said, "and you're all plenty tired. But you began to look a little more like a hockey team."

Danny and Rick looked at one another and smiled briefly.

"We've got a tough game coming up tomorrow night," the coach went on. "I want every one of you to be home and in bed by 9:30 tonight."

"Well," Danny said later. "That means we'll have to make our youth group meeting roll right along. And we'll probably have to cancel that committee meeting afterward. We couldn't possibly get through with all of that and still get home by 9:30."

"Do you mean to tell me that you're going to pay attention to that guff about turning in at 9:30?" Rick asked him. "None of the guys'll be in bed by that time and Masters knows it."

"But he's the coach," Danny replied. "And when we went out for hockey we promised to follow his training rules. We ought to be in bed by the time he told us to, whether any of the rest of the team does or not."

"But if he does check he won't go into the church basement," Rick countered. "He'll go down to the theater and the hamburger joints and the bowling alleys like he did once during the football season."

"I'm not thinking about getting caught," Danny answered, "or even getting the rest, which I know we'll all need if we're going to win that game tomorrow night. But what about our Christian testimonies? What would people think of our Lord if they saw that we don't act any differently than the guys who don't even claim to be Christians?"

For half a minute Rick walked in silence. "You know, there's a lot more to this Christian business than a guy would think."

"That's for sure," Danny replied seriously. "It's like Kay says, if we want our friends to become Christians, we've got to remember that they're watching us and comparing what we are with what they think a Christian ought to be."

"When you put it that way, I guess it does make a difference whether we keep the training rules."

They were almost at the Barber house where Danny roomed when Rick remembered and asked Danny about going to the movie with him and Marilyn.

"You could get Kay and we could have a malt and a sandwich afterward. It would be a lot of fun."

"The malt and sandwich idea is good," Danny said, "only why don't we go over to church instead?"

"I asked Marilyn about that but she won't miss that movie. She'll go with me to Bible Club though if I take her to the movie Sunday night. Why don't you and Kay come along?"

Danny stopped and leaned against a shaggy oak tree on the corner. "We'd like to be with you and Marilyn Sunday night," he said gently. "But you know that we don't go to movies."

"That's right, I remember now." Rick's smile faded. "But why, Danny? Just what's wrong with going to a movie?"

Danny gulped. "I don't know what a preacher'd say. But the only thing I can tell you is why I don't go." He kicked into the snow with his boot. "Can you remember anything about the last movie you went to?"

"Sure. It was only last night. But what's that got to do with it?"

"Was there any smoking in it?"

"A guy can see that on the streets every day."

"Was there any drinking?"

"A little. It was the funniest thing when that guy got drunk and fell downstairs and–" When he saw the look on Danny's face he stopped. "I–I guess it wasn't so funny after all," he said lamely. "Not really funny, I mean."

"What was the plot about?"

"Oh, the usual thing. A really rich guy who ran around in a fancy foreign car and never worked or anything started going with this pretty girl while his wife was away. Only she didn't know he was married and–"

"Was there anything in it that glorified Christ? Was there anything that would make you want to live a better life?"

Rick shook his head.

"But it sounded like there was a lot in it that might make a guy want to sin, especially if he happened to be a little weak," Danny said. "That's the reason I don't go to movies."

Mrs. Barber came out on the porch just then and called Danny to supper.

"You think about what I've said, Rick."

The other boy was troubled a little by Danny's testimony regarding movies after he went to bed that night. But he still couldn't see that there was too much wrong with them. After all, most of the kids went to movies, except Kay and Danny and a few other church kids. He was sure he could never get Marilyn to give them up. She had to see every one. By the time he drifted off to sleep he had assembled a good line of arguments to give to Danny the next day. Still, when he awakened in the morning, a vague uneasiness bothered him.

The hockey game that night was bitterly fought. Edgemont came to town, the favorites by at least three goals. And the first stanza looked as though that estimate was conservative. Before Cedarton realized what was happening, the ace Edgemont wing eluded the defensemen and twice slammed the puck into the net behind the goalie.

"Well," the Edgemont player grinned cockily, "I guess that'll hold you guys for a while."

"Not bad," Danny told him.

"I'll say it wasn't bad," the guy went on. "But I'll tell you what, we'll try to hold the score down as much as we can."

Danny watched the guy intently out of the corner of his eye as he took the puck from one of his teammates and began to skate toward Rick. The other wing skated by, wide open, and shouted for the puck, but the opposing star only feinted toward him. With a brilliant fake Danny eluded Rick and skated toward the goalie, handling the puck like a veteran. His long, rifle-like shot came within an inch of going in. It brought a gasp of approval from the crowd.

"Call time out," Danny whispered to Rick, who was acting captain. "I think I know how to stop him."

When the team had all gathered around, Danny said, "That guy's a grandstander. He won't pass to anyone else on their team after he gets down close enough to where he might be able to make a goal himself. When he gets down there let's put three guys on him. We'll crowd him so close he won't even be able to keep his stick on the puck."

The first time they tried it the Edgemont wing eluded two Cedarton men cleverly, but he couldn't get by Rick. The acting captain worked in from the side and stole the puck neatly. He whipped the puck out to the center, and a smooth passing game ended only when Danny snaked the puck past the end of the goalie's stick to score.

Two minutes later the Edgemont flash started toward the goal. Three Cedarton men swarmed in to crowd him until he got tangled with the puck and skated over it. From then on, they bottled him so tightly that he didn't make another goal. Cedarton squeaked past Edgemont by a single point.

"Oh, that was a wonderful game," Marilyn said excitedly to Rick as they crowded into the shop and waited for a booth. "I never saw anything so thrilling. Dad says we've got a good chance to win the state championship."

"We aren't even sure of being in the state tourney," Rick countered. "I wouldn't predict a state championship."

Everyone was talking loudly and excitedly in the booths around them, but for some reason that strange uneasiness came back to Rick.

"Now what's the matter with you?" she asked. "You look like you'd just lost your best friend, if you ever had one."

"I was just thinking."

"Don't do that. You might strain something."

A booth emptied just then and they sat down across from one another. After they had ordered, Rick put the menu behind the napkin holder and said, "Seriously, Marilyn, I was wondering if we couldn't skip the movie Sunday night."

"But why?"

"So we could go to church with Danny and Kay. We could go out and have a malt afterward."

The smile left her face. "Listen, Rick Haines, if you think I'm going to quit movies just so I can go to that stuffy old church of yours, you've got another guess coming!"

CHAPTER 11

AN INVITATION

Danny Orlis was the last one in the shower when the game was over. Everyone else, except the team manager and the janitor, had gone when he finally got dressed and met Kay in the vestibule in front of the schoolhouse.

"Hi, Kay!" he said hurrying up to her. "I got out of there as fast as I could."

"I've just been standing here trying to get back down to earth after that game. It just took my breath away."

Danny laughed. "If you think it was exciting from where you were, how do you think it was where I was?"

They went out into the chill night air and started up the sidewalk toward the shop.

"Did you see Rick and Marilyn?" he asked her.

"They went out quite a while ago," she replied.

"I wish we could have talked with them. I'm worried about Rick."

Kay nodded understandingly.

"He's accepted the Lord as his Savior all right," Danny went on, "but there are so many things he doesn't understand yet."

"Like what?"

They waited for a car to pass.

"Living a devoted life mainly. Rick wants to live like a good Christian, but he doesn't know anything about the Bible. He's confused about what he ought to do and what he shouldn't."

"Marilyn won't be much help, I'm afraid. As long as he keeps going out with her, she's going to have him taking her to movies and dances and places like that."

"She told him that she won't go to Bible Club with him Monday night if he doesn't take her to the movie Sunday." Briefly, Danny told Kay how he had talked with Rick about movies. "But I don't think I got very far."

"It goes to prove that it would be better for Christian guys and girls not to date unsaved kids."

"Do you suppose we could get them to go with us some place tomorrow night?" Danny asked.

"Maybe we could talk to them about the Lord. Maybe we could get hold of Marilyn."

They walked into the shop and spied Marilyn and Rick sitting in a booth.

"You're not going to make that kind of a Christian out of me, Richard Haines," Marilyn was saying, her shrill voice carrying across the store. "So you can just as well quit right now."

"There they are, Danny," Kay said.

Danny had caught the glint of fire in Marilyn's manner and the concern and embarrassment written on his friend's face. He tried to stop Kay. But she had already reached the couple sitting in the booth.

"Hi, guys! Wasn't that a wonderful game?"

"It sure was," Rick muttered without enthusiasm.

Marilyn stared straight ahead.

"What is this?" Danny asked easily. "A private fight or can anyone get in?"

"I don't know," Rick told him, grinning crookedly. "But I'd like to get out of it. I can tell you that."

"He's been preaching at me all evening. I'm getting tired of it."

"Now, it's not as bad as all that," Kay said gently.

The waitress came up just then and they gave their orders. When she was gone, Danny and Kay switched the subject to the hockey game. In a few minutes Marilyn was laughing again.

They were still eating when a tall, husky stranger wearing a heavy red-letter sweater emblazoned with a white *E* approached their booth.

"Hi, guys!" he said warmly. "Haven't we met some place before?"

"Sure thing," Danny and Rick replied almost at the same time. "You came within an inch of whipping us tonight."

"It was a good game," the stranger said. "You guys have a great team."

"Thanks," Rick answered.

"You know," the other guy went on, "we've got a big Youth for Christ meeting over in Edgemont tomorrow night." He laid a small, attractive card on the table. "Why don't you guys come over?"

Danny looked over at Rick quizzically.

"I think I can get Dad's car," Rick said, "if you'd all like to go."

"It sounds like fun," Kay put in quickly.

"You can count on me," Danny added.

For an instant or two Marilyn toyed with her ice cream. "If all the rest of you are going, I guess maybe I can go too."

"Great," the Edgemont hockey player said. "I'll be looking for you. Maybe you can come over to our house with everyone afterward. We all get together and listen to music and have sandwiches after the rally."

"Good deal," Danny said.

When the Edgemont hockey player had left, Marilyn pushed back her ice cream dish and laid down her spoon determinedly. "Well," she retorted, "that sounds like a fine way to spend a Saturday night."

"It sure does," Rick replied.

When Danny left Kay at the door to her rooming house she said, "Don't forget to pray for Marilyn."

"Sure thing."

Danny Orlis was more tired after the game than he had realized and he slept until almost 10 o'clock the next morning. Kirk and Karen Barber had had breakfast and had gone out almost two hours before he finally came downstairs.

"Good morning, Mrs. Barber," he said. "Did you think I was going to sleep all day?"

"I was beginning to," she got up wearily and started for the refrigerator. "I'll fix you some hot chocolate and toast."

"It's only a little while until dinner now," said Danny.

She closed the refrigerator and dropped slowly into a nearby chair. With her reddened, care-worn hand she pushed her straggling, graying hair back from her eyes.

"What's the matter, Mrs. Barber?" Danny asked.

"Nothing."

He came over and sat down across the table from her. "Now I know better. When my mom gets to looking like you, there's usually something wrong."

"I–I–" Then she stopped short. "I'm sorry that I lied to you, Danny. There is something wrong – something terribly wrong. But I don't want to burden you with it. There isn't anything you can do."

"How do you know?"

She bit her lip nervously. "I had a phone call from the man who owns this house," she said. "He–he's been renting it to us for years. He even rented it to us before my husband died. But now he's decided that he wants to sell."

"What's so terrible about that?"

"It is serious, Danny," she exclaimed. "I don't have any money to buy the house. We'll have to move, but there isn't a suitable place for rent in town."

Danny gulped hard as he saw the tears welling in her eyes. "We'll just have to put our trust in the Lord."

***

Rick got his dad's car that night and took Marilyn, Danny, and Kay over to the Youth for Christ meeting in Edgemont.

The speaker, a young minister from Minneapolis, brought a powerful message, but Marilyn had steeled herself against him. She sat silently through the singing. Her lips were pressed tightly together and her eyes were staring off into space.

When the time came for the invitation she stood with the others. Her hands clenched the top of the seat in front of her until her knuckles showed white. Kay saw it and touched Marilyn appealingly on the arm. She jerked savagely away. When the meeting was finally over, the others wanted to go to Bill Dawson's house with the Edgemont group, but Marilyn refused flatly.

"You can go on if you want to," she snapped, "but I've got a busting headache. I'm staying in the car."

The foursome in the car were strangely quiet as they drove over the snow-covered road to Cedarton.

Two or three times Kay or Danny tried to start a conversation, but it did no good.

"Wasn't that a wonderful message?" Kay asked on one occasion.

"I didn't see anything so wonderful about it,"

Marilyn retorted angrily. "In fact the whole evening was one big bore. I've been trying to figure out why on earth I ever came along."

With that she flounced into the far corner of the front seat and sat there pouting. When they drove into town she insisted that Rick let her off first.

Rick had supposed that Marilyn would be in the same mood when he called for her Sunday evening, but she wasn't.

"I–I'm sorry about last night," he said.

"Last night was last night," she said as she got into her coat. "We're going to have a wonderful time tonight at the movie. I just know it."

"Yeh," he replied without enthusiasm.

Marilyn chattered happily as they walked down to the theater and bought their tickets. This time he was the one who was silent. He knew what he ought to do. He – grimly he forced such thoughts from his mind and stepped into the lobby behind her.

Butch Winston, one of the hockey team, was working there. "If it isn't preacher Haines!" he exclaimed. "What are you doing here?"

"Can't I come to a movie if I want to, wise guy?"

"Sure, sure. Only after that sermon you gave us about being a Christian I never expected to see you here again."

Rick stopped short, as though he had been slapped.

"Come on," Marilyn took him by the arm. "Don't pay any attention to him. Let's get a seat before the movie starts."

CHAPTER 12

THE TEST

That Sunday evening Danny picked up Kay from her house and they walked to church together.

"Why so solemn?" he asked her. "You act like your best friend ran away with the family fortune."

"I've been terribly concerned for Rick and Marilyn, Danny."

"I phoned him this afternoon. Thought maybe I'd get another chance to talk to him about going to the movie tonight. But he said he had some studies he had to get done."

"If only we could make him see what this fooling around with the world can do to his testimony!"

"We've got to remember that Rick hasn't been a Christian very long," Danny replied. "We can't expect him to understand about separation the way we do. We'll just have to pray harder than ever for him."

***

Meanwhile Rick Haines was standing in the lobby of the theater, staring into the darkened building.

"What's the matter, Rick?" Butch taunted. "Did all that fancy religion of yours wear out already?"

So that was what Butch thought! That was what any of the guys who saw him there would be thinking!

Marilyn took his arm and whispered to him impatiently, "Let's go and sit down. Everybody's watching us."

She took a step toward the aisle. He hung back, his head spinning.

"Rick!" she said louder than before. "Come on!"

Two or three near the aisle in the back rows turned to stare at them.

"Make up your mind," Butch taunted. "Are you going to go sit down or not?"

Another couple came into the theater just then, and Butch waved Rick and Marilyn aside so they could take their seats.

"Rick Haines!" Marilyn whispered angrily. "Are you going down front with me or not?"

Slowly, reluctantly, he shook his head.

For a brief instant she stared at him, eyes blazing, she said, "If you don't go in with me now, we're through! I'll never go anywhere with you again."

"I–I'm sorry, Marilyn," he stammered. He turned quickly and hurried out of the theater.

***

They were singing the last song before the evening message when Rick came into the church and sat down beside Danny and Kay. Danny looked over at him and smiled.

"I'm so glad you changed your mind, Rick," Kay said when the service was over, "and didn't go to the movie after all."

"I don't know what came over me," he told her. "I shouldn't have left Marilyn in the lurch like that. She'll never speak to me again. And I don't blame her. But I–I just couldn't go into that theater."

Danny nodded understandingly.

The next morning Rick called Marilyn's home. She hung up on him.

"I don't want to hear anything you've got to say, Rick Haines," she said icily. "Now or ever!" There was grim finality in her tone as she hung up.

Later that morning he met her in the corridor between classes, but she turned haughtily away.

"She's got a right to be mad though," he confided to Danny at noon. "That was the worst trick a guy could ever pull on a girl. She'll never get over it."

"She will when she trusts Christ as her Savior," Danny told him. "You didn't make your mistake in refusing to go to the movie with her. You made it in waiting so long to decide you weren't going to."

"I don't know," Rick said bitterly. "It seems like I've been in one mess after another since I became a Christian."

"Things will work out for you. Just keep on trusting."

The guys reported for hockey practice after school, but Coach Masters called off the Monday session.

"You guys played a good, hard, solid game," he said. "You deserve a rest." He paused for a moment and looked from one to another.

"I'm going to share this with you," he went on. "Because it might be just the incentive you need to put forth the extra effort that wins games. Clarinda is it as far as this year is concerned. If we beat them we'll get the number one seeded spot in the regional tourney and have a very good chance to win the State."

A ripple of surprise swept the players.

"Now I want you guys to take it easy this afternoon," he concluded. "Forget all about hockey until tomorrow night. And then come down here determined to give it everything you've got, and more too."

Most of the guys gathered in clusters about the locker room talking excitedly, but Danny and Rick left at once and walked home.

"Maybe I can get out and sell some magazines between now and supper time," Danny said. "I could sure use a little extra money."

"Who couldn't?"

"I'll stop by for you tonight for Bible Club."

"I'm not sure that I'll be going."

"Why, of course you're going. We've all got to be out for every single meeting if we're going to get this club launched and growing."

"You can get along without me."

"I'll be after you, about 7:15."

Danny had been a little afraid that Rick wouldn't go to Bible Club that night. But when he stopped at his friend's house a little after seven, Rick was ready to go.

"I've been doing a lot of thinking since I left you this afternoon," Rick said. "It doesn't make much difference whether Marilyn and I get to be good friends again or not. The important thing is that she needs Christ as her Savior."

"You've got something there."

"I know it won't do any good for me to try to talk to her now. She wouldn't listen. Do you suppose Kay would go and see her? She could explain things better than I can."

"I know she would."

Kay was eager to talk with Marilyn when the two boys approached her about it after the Bible Club meeting. "I don't know whether I can do any good or not, but if you'll pray for me I'll certainly try."

Danny walked with her as far as the corner west of Marilyn's and left her to go up to the house alone. "I'll call you as soon as I get home and tell you how things go," she told him.

Marilyn came to the door, red-eyed and somber. For an instant or so she looked at Kay belligerently.

"We missed you tonight."

"I didn't miss going." Nevertheless she led Kay into the house and asked her to sit down before the big, modern fireplace.

Marilyn was biting her lips nervously. Finally she got to her feet and walked slowly to the fireplace where she turned and faced Kay.

"I know why you came!" she blurted suddenly. "And I can tell you right now that it isn't going to do any good! I'm going to live my own life! *I'm not going to be a Christian!*"

Marilyn Forester stood before the fireplace, her dark eyes snapping defiance. "I know why you came over here tonight, Kay, and I can tell you now that you can save your breath."

Kay was staring into the dying embers in the fireplace.

"Why do you think I came?"

"Rick asked you to talk to me about becoming a Christian. Didn't he?"

"He was terribly sorry about what happened in the theater lobby the other night. And he is concerned about–"

"I should think he would be," Marilyn cut in. "I was never so embarrassed in my life. He left me right in the theater aisle, in front of all those people." Tears welled up in her eyes. "I'm a laughingstock at school. I'll never be able to live it down."

"Rick shouldn't have left you," Kay said. "He knows now that he shouldn't even have promised to take you to the movie."

"He'll never get another chance to leave me like that again. You can tell him that for me."

Kay felt the hem on her coat. What would her mom say to a person like Marilyn? Silently she prayed for help.

"The important thing is whether you listen when God tries to talk to you, when He tries to tell you that you are a sinner in need of a Savior."

Marilyn crossed over to a chair and sat down. "I'm not ready to be a Christian."

"I know just how you feel. You want to live your life in your own way. Isn't that right?"

"What's so wrong about that?"

"Just about everything. When we say that, we act as though God can't be trusted with our lives. Any Christian who's really living for Christ can tell you that he's a thousand times happier with the Lord in control than he was when he tried to blunder along on his own."

"All I've ever heard from Christians is 'don't do this and don't do that.' I want to have some fun while I'm young."

"Don't you think Danny and Rick and I and the other Christians at school have any fun?"

"Well, I–I don't know," Marilyn replied. "You never go to a movie or a dance or have our kind of fun."

"That might be," Kay went on, "but if you'd join us at Bible Club and youth group, you'd find out that we have plenty of fun. Sure, there are things that we don't do any more now that we're Christians, but that's no sign we don't enjoy ourselves." She leaned forward earnestly, "Won't you trust Christ as your Savior, Marilyn?"

She sat there stiffly, "I'm not ready yet."

Kay took her New Testament from her pocket, but there were heavy footsteps on the porch. Marilyn's dad came in.

"Hey, it's cold outside tonight," he said, stamping the snow from his heavy boots and slapping his hands together. "It'll be 20 below tonight."

Marilyn got up quickly. "Come on, Kay," she said, "let's go out in the kitchen and make some sandwiches and cocoa."

Reluctantly, the missionary's daughter put her Bible away.

A transformation seemed to come over Marilyn. Where she had been somber and on the verge of tears a moment before, she now suddenly became happy. She chattered excitedly and began to laugh. Kay was heartsick when she finally went home.

"The only thing I know of that would possibly do any good," she said the next day after telling Danny what had happened, "is to be as friendly as I can and try to reach her that way."

"I suppose you're right."

"She's under conviction. It's easy to see that. But she just doesn't want to yield to Christ."

Danny prayed for Marilyn and Kay as he promised, but he didn't get to see much of either of them the next few days. The hockey team was putting in long hours on the ice in preparation for the Clarinda game. The papers were already calling the game the preview of the State Tournament. Excitement was building up to a fever pitch.

"We've scouted Clarinda thoroughly," Coach Masters told the players, "and to be honest with you they don't have a weak spot on their team. Their goalie is one of the cleverest I've ever seen in high school hockey. And their defensemen give him tremendous support."

He spent the first two days sharpening the defense. He and one of the other coaches who had played hockey in college joined the second string and did their best to score with Clarinda plays. However, Butch Winston at the goal and the two defensemen did a commendable job of smothering the attack.

"If you guys play like that Friday night," Coach Masters said when the session ended, "we'll have a very good chance to set Clarinda back on her heels. A very good chance."

"We'll sure do our best," Butch beamed.

"Fine," the coach told him. "Now I want all of you guys out early tomorrow night. We're going to brush up on those new plays and round out our practice for this game. We'll scrimmage tomorrow night and just warm up Thursday. I want you all out and ready to go to work early tomorrow."

"Hey," Butch said to Danny as they crowded into the shower room, "I can hardly wait for that game Friday night!"

The next afternoon the guys hurried, laughing and jostling, into the locker room and began to change into their hockey clothes. Usually the coach was in the locker room waiting for them, but that day only the team manager was there.

"Did you know they're going to have an all-afternoon pep rally tomorrow?" Butch asked Danny. "It's going to be a big deal."

Before he could say more, the door opened and the coach came striding into the locker room. His face was set in a grim, hard line and his eyes were flashing. He stopped in the middle of the floor and stared, first at one excited, noisy knot of players and then at another. Under his blazing stare the laughter faded from their faces and they fell silent. For almost a minute he stared at them until the little room was breathless.

"I had a most disturbing visit a few minutes ago," he began coldly. "The sort of visit I never thought I would have here in Cedarton."

He turned slowly to face Danny and Butch.

"I had a call this afternoon from a businessman who is a good friend of high school sports," the coach went on; "a man who knows what is expected of an athlete; a man who is as interested as we are in seeing Cedarton go into the State Tourney. He came to me with the disturbing story that some of you guys are breaking training."

The players looked at one another quickly. The color drained from Butch Winston's face.

"I–I wonder who he could be talking about?" he whispered hoarsely.

"This businessman said that he saw two guys on the team out after hours and smoking," Coach Masters continued. "He saw them Saturday night, Monday night, and last night."

Danny looked over at Butch, who was biting his lip savagely.

"You guys all know what our training rules are," the coach said. "And you know what the penalty is for breaking them. You may think that this game Friday night is so important that we can't afford to get along without you. But no victory is that important. I would rather play guys who obey training regulations and lose every game than to win the State Championship with those who don't."

He hesitated while the bell sounded four o'clock.

"Winston," he said when it was quiet again, "and Ross, you're through for the season. Turn in your uniforms."

"Do–do you mean we're not going to play anymore at all?" Butch asked plaintively.

"That's right," the coach snapped.

"But I–I didn't smoke hardly any at all," Ross protested. "And I wasn't out late at night. Isn't there something else we could do? Isn't there some other punishment you could give us?"

"You were seen on three different occasions as late as 1:15, Ross," the instructor replied, "and you were smoking all three times. You knew our training rules, and you knew the penalty for breaking them. Does that answer your question?"

"But coach," the team manager put in weakly, "Butch is our starting goalie and Ross is our best defenseman. Clarinda will cut us to shreds if they don't get to play."

"They should have thought of that before," Coach Masters said. "You stay in here and check in their equipment. And come on, the rest of you. We've really got a job ahead of us."

The guys went out on the ice soberly and stood waiting for the coach to direct them.

They went through the motions of a practice that night, but it was strained and unnatural. There wasn't another goalie in school who could begin to come up to Winston, and Ross had been in line for all-conference honors for his play at defense.

Coach Masters was worried too. Danny could see that by the way he shifted first one player and then another.

"Did you ever play defense, Orlis?" he asked Danny toward the end of the long practice period.

The young woodsman nodded. "A guy has to play everything up where I come from."

"Fine," he said. "We'll try you there tomorrow night. We'll have to have a short scrimmage tomorrow night, gang. We've got some big problems to work out."

Rick and Danny dressed silently when practice was over and walked home together. "Hey, that's sure rough for the team, isn't it?" said Rick.

Danny nodded. "But the coach couldn't do anything else."

Rick kicked a piece of ice along the sidewalk. "You know," he said suddenly, "it's a good thing I'm a Christian."

"How's that?" Danny asked.

"I used to run with Butch and Ross all the time, he continued. "I'd have been in on that deal too if the Lord hadn't gotten hold of me and straightened me out."

Danny was silent for a long while. "You make me feel a little guilty," he said at last. "If we'd worked a little harder to reach Butch and Ross this might not have happened at all."

CHAPTER 13

EXTRA PRACTICE

The story of what had happened on the hockey team the night before spread like a prairie fire over the school. The kids were furious.

"Here we had the best chance we've ever had for a State Championship," one of the guys said to Butch in the halls, "and you guys had to go and spoil it."

"It was Orlis," Butch defended sullenly. "He squealed on us. That's what he did. If it hadn't been for him, we'd have been all right."

"You mean Danny squealed on you?" the other student repeated. "You mean he actually went to the coach and squealed?"

"Sure thing," Butch said. "And just wait until I catch him out alone. I'll teach him!"

Don Ross came up to them. "Listen, Butch," he said softly. "Don't blame Danny or anyone else. We knew what the training rules were, but we broke them. We don't have anyone else to blame but ourselves."

The color crept up into Butch's cheeks and he turned hurriedly and rushed down the corridor.

Right after lunch that day the student body gathered in the assembly hall for the pep rally, but Coach Masters and his staff took the hockey squad down on the ice.

"We've got a lot of work to do," he said, "to get into shape for tomorrow night."

In the next two hours he completely reshuffled the team. He brought up the third-string goalie, switched Rick to Danny's wing spot, and put Danny back on defense.

"We've got to stop Clarinda's scoring attack," he told the boys grimly. "If we can do that, we've still got a good chance of beating them."

Danny and the new goalie tried hard enough, but the second team, using Clarinda's fast breaking attack, was still able to knife through for three goals in two furious periods. Coach Masters gave up working on the new offensive plays and spent all the remaining time on defense, but the team was ragged and jittery. Finally he called the practice to a halt and sent the squad to the showers.

"I guess that'll have to do," he said wearily. "Get to bed early tonight and get plenty of rest. We've got a big job to do tomorrow night."

"I don't know," Danny said as he and Rick walked home together. "I just can't seem to get the hang of that position yet."

"You didn't look so bad."

"Don't kid me. I was awful out there tonight."

Danny went up to bed at the usual time that night, but he couldn't sleep for thinking about the hockey game they would be playing the following night. Sometime after 11 o'clock, the wind came up until it howled under the eaves and shrieked through the pines just outside his window. He got up once or twice to look out, shivering in the cold. The ice was so thick on the glass that he couldn't see whether it was snowing or not.

The next morning when he got up, however, he saw that the sidewalks and streets were choked with drifts, and fine new snow was still swirling down.

"There won't be any school today," Kirk chirped happily as he saw Danny on the stairs. "There won't be any school today."

"There won't be any hockey game tonight either," he replied. Somehow he felt real relief that the game would have to be canceled or postponed.

Along in the middle of the morning it quit snowing, and at noon Danny plowed through the drifts to school. They weren't holding classes and only a small handful of kids had ventured out.

"They're going to cancel the game, Danny," Rick said when he stomped into the schoolhouse. They're going to cancel it because there's a good chance that we'll meet Clarinda in the Regional Tournament."

"That's all right. That'll give us time enough to work on our new positions a little more. And believe me, we can use it."

"You can say that again," Tommy Willis, the third-string goalie exclaimed fervently.

The following Monday at practice the squad asked for a chance to talk to Coach Masters.

"A-and so," Rick, who had been elected spokesman, concluded, "we thought maybe you'd reconsider and let Butch and Don Ross play with us in the tournament."

For a moment the coach's eyes snapped, but when he spoke his voice was emotionless. "We have never made an exception to the penalty for breaking our training rules."

"But this is different," Rick countered.

"I fail to see that, guys," he answered evenly. "I will talk it over with my assistants and with the principal and superintendent, but I think you know my feelings, even though we lose the game."

That night was Bible Club, and Kay got Marilyn Forester to go with her. "I shouldn't go at all," Marilyn said reluctantly. "I've got a lot of studying to do."

There were 30 or 40 kids out for Bible Club that night, but it seemed as though the lesson was just for Marilyn. She squirmed uncomfortably, and as soon as the meeting was over she got her coat and hurried out. Kay almost had to run to catch her.

"You won't catch me going there again and listening to that silly stuff," she snorted on the way home. Nevertheless, she pushed aside her lessons and asked Kay questions about the Bible and the new birth for almost an hour after they reached her home.

"You know, Kay," she said as the missionary's daughter got ready to leave, "I wish you were rooming here at our house. Stop by for me on the way to school tomorrow, will you?"

For the next ten days the two girls were inseparable. Marilyn attended church with Kay and once she even went to prayer meeting.

Marilyn knew from the very beginning about the missionary from Mexico who was speaking at the Women's Missionary Society on that Thursday afternoon.

"But I can't get to see her because she's speaking at Edgemont at a banquet tonight and will be leaving here before school gets out," Kay said.

"Perhaps you can manage to see her at noon," Marilyn sympathized. "After all, if she knows your mom and just saw her a couple of weeks ago you ought to get a chance to talk to her."

Kay had really thought she would get a chance to see the missionary at noon. She and Marilyn had hurried to Marilyn's home to phone as soon as they had finished eating, but Miss Davis wasn't expected until two o'clock.

"You've just got to see her," Marilyn said.

Kay choked back the disappointment.

"I'll fix things," Marilyn exclaimed.

"What are you going to do?" Kay asked.

"I'll call the school and tell them you're sick."

"Do you think that would work?" Kay asked hesitantly.

"Sure it will." Quickly Marilyn dialed the number.

CHAPTER 14

RIGHT LIVING COUNTS

"**I** don't know whether we ought to do that or not, Marilyn," Kay said hesitantly. "I–"

"Don't be silly," Marilyn told her. "I've done this lots of times." She turned back to the telephone quickly as the school secretary answered.

"This is Mrs. Barnes," she said crisply. "I've called to tell you that Kay Milburn won't be in school this afternoon. She has a terrible headache. She stays with us, you know. Thank you." Marilyn turned back to her friend as she hung up the phone.

"There," she said triumphantly, "it's all fixed. You can go to the missionary meeting this afternoon and you won't be getting an unexcused absence either."

Kay got up and walked across the room. "We've lied to them," she said nervously. "I'm not sick at all."

"Well, you would have been if you hadn't gotten to go to the church to hear that missionary speaker."

She started to put on her coat. "Say, if you'd call out there for me I wouldn't have to go to school this afternoon either. I could go and hear the missionary too."

"Oh, but I couldn't do that," Kay protested. "I couldn't lie to them."

Marilyn snorted disdainfully. "It was all right for me to lie for you though."

The missionary's daughter walked slowly back to the chair where she had put her coat and slipped into it. Her face was flushed crimson and her lips were trembling.

After all, it was the only chance she'd get to see Miss Jensen and find out firsthand how her mom and Danny's Aunt Mabel were. It was her only chance to talk with someone who had been back in Mexico recently. And she was so homesick, there were times when she didn't see how she could stand it.

She walked out of the house and down the brick steps. At the walk she hesitated momentarily, then turned and shuffled dejectedly toward the church. She tried hard to force the nagging thoughts of what she had just done out of her mind.

The church was across town from where Marilyn lived and by the time Kay got there the meeting was ready to begin. A slim, graying woman with distinctive clothing was sitting on the platform.

"What's the program today?" Kay whispered to the woman who was sitting next to her.

"Miss Tompkins is going to tell us about her field in Guatemala," her neighbor replied.

"But–but I thought a Miss Alice Jensen from Mexico was going to be the speaker," Kay protested.

"Somebody said she took ill, suddenly," the woman said. "But I think Miss Tompkins will be just as interesting. She's going to tell about the Communists over there and how they are affecting the missionary efforts."

"I–I see," Kay stammered. She had let Marilyn lie to get her out of school and Miss Jensen hadn't even been there. Suddenly she realized what she had done. And she had been trying to talk with Marilyn about her soul. What chance could she have to win her to the Lord now?

Her eyes burning with tears she got to her feet and stumbled outside. The raw March wind was swirling through the naked trees and stinging her face, but she scarcely felt it as she walked along the sidewalk toward home. Somehow, she managed to get back to Mrs. Barnes' and up to her room, where she threw herself, sobbing, across the bed.

***

Back at school Coach Masters called the hockey squad together at one corner of the rink.

"You guys came to me with a request," he said seriously, "and I told you I would take it up with my assistants and the school authorities."

The team tensed expectantly.

"We have had two meetings trying to decide whether we should permit Butch Winston and Don Ross to play with us during the balance of the year," he went on.

He stopped momentarily and moistened his lips. "We decided this afternoon that it wouldn't be fair to the guys who had kept the training rules to let them play. Neither would it be fair to those who might follow their example and break training too, if we do not enforce the penalties for breaking training."

A low moan went up from several of the players.

"I know we need them," he continued. "We need them badly. But we don't need them badly enough to let them play under the present circumstances." With that he skated out on the ice and blew his whistle. "Come on, guys, let's get at it. We've got a lot of work to do."

"I'll say we have," Rick muttered under his breath to Danny.

That practice went better than usual. Tommy Willis was getting a little confidence as goalie and fended off half a dozen blistering angle shots, the kind any goalie will miss once in a while. And Danny was mastering his position as defenseman. He wasn't such a sucker for faking as he had been the first two or three nights. And he made several plays back in dangerous territory that brought a gasp of praise from the little knot of fans in the stands.

"But still we've got a long way to go," Danny said to Rick when the practice was over.

"You can say that again," Rick replied fervently.

Kay had planned on going to youth group with Danny that night. But she called him after supper and told him that she wouldn't be going. Her eyes were red and swollen, and the pain was growing in her heart until she knew she couldn't sit through a meeting.

As she tried to pray she knew what she had to do. She got up and put on her robe and went down into the living room where Mrs. Barnes was sitting.

"I–I have something I want to tell you."

"Yes, Kay."

"Marilyn called the school this noon and–and told them she was you and that I was sick," Kay blurted. "I don't know why I let her do it, but I wanted you to know I'm–I'm terribly sorry."

"I'm so glad you talked with me," the older woman said gently. "You see the school called me to check on it. I was wondering when you would come and tell me about it."

"I'm awfully sorry," Kay repeated. With that the floodgates broke and Kay sank, sobbing, into a chair across from Mrs. Barnes.

The older woman got up and put her arm about Kay's shoulder. "Let's talk to the Lord about this. You know that He's quick to forgive."

Together they knelt in prayer.

Kay tried that night to get hold of Marilyn but she didn't answer, and she couldn't reach her the next morning either. When Kay got to school she went directly to the principal's office and asked to see Mr. Reimer.

"Well," he said curtly, "what have you to say for yourself?"

"I want to tell you how sorry I am that I–I lied and skipped school yesterday afternoon," she stammered. "I'm a Christian and I–I know I shouldn't have done it. I knew it at the time. I didn't act like a Christian should and I–I'm so ashamed."

Mr. Reimer looked at her strangely. "I've been a teacher for 25 years," he said at last, "and this is the first time anything like this ever happened to me. I'm going to give you an excuse for yesterday." He sat down and wrote out a blue slip. "If we had more like you out here, Kay," he concluded, "our problems would be a lot less."

She smiled weakly. "It isn't that I'm any different than any of the other kids, Mr. Reimer," she said. "It's only that I'm a Christian and trying to live as Jesus would have me live." The smile faded. "But I didn't act like a Christian yesterday."

From there she went to the classes she had skipped and told the teachers what had happened and asked their forgiveness.

"Now," she said, "if I can just talk to Marilyn, I'll have everything fixed."

But it wasn't so simple to get a chance to talk to her friend. Marilyn was in the pep club and had a meeting that noon to work on a skit for a rally they were holding before the hockey team left for the regional tournament.

She thought she would get a chance to see Marilyn after school, but the pep club went to Clarinda too, so she had to wait until later.

Danny and the team drew Clarinda in the opening round of the tournament and went out on the ice nervously at the start of the game. Clarinda was keyed for the contest. They came slashing down the rink like professionals to fake past Danny and score between Tommy's legs almost in a matter of seconds.

Not that Cedarton didn't battle back with all that they had. They fought furiously and for a brief instant midway in the third period they led by a single goal. But Clarinda came slashing back to take the lead and hold it. A valiant, exhausted Cedarton team skated wearily off the ice at the close of the contest.

"I'm proud of you, guys," Coach Masters said warmly in the locker room. "I'm prouder of you tonight than I've ever been, even when you've won."

"We could have made it if we'd only had Don and Butch," one of the guys blurted bitterly.

"The way you guys played tonight," the coach said, "I don't think Don and Butch would have made any difference. You gave everything you had. That's all anybody can do."

That night Kay happened to be in the shop when the first carload of the pep club got back into town. Marilyn saw her alone in a booth and sat with her.

"Hi," she said, "long time no see."

"That's right," Kay grinned crookedly. "I've been trying to see you, though. I–I've been wanting to talk to you."

". . . And so," Kay concluded almost tearfully, "I want to ask your forgiveness too."

"My forgiveness?" Marilyn echoed. "It was my idea in the first place. I'm the one who got you into the mess. You don't have to ask my forgiveness."

"But I shouldn't have let you do it. I–I'm a Christian, Marilyn. I should act like one. And I–I certainly didn't when I let you lie for me."

Marilyn was quiet for a long while. "Does being a Christian mean that much to you?" she asked hoarsely.

Kay nodded. A tear hung on her eyelash, then rolled silently down her cheek.

"You know, Kay," Marilyn said huskily, "I've been fighting the Lord all along. I've kidded myself into thinking that I'm just as good as you are. But I see now that–that–" she gulped hard. "Kay, would you explain the way of salvation to me again, please?"

For almost a minute the girls sat staring at one another. The shop was rapidly becoming a hive of noise as the hockey game crowd funneled in, but neither of the girls noticed. Marilyn leaned forward earnestly.

"You–you mean you want to hear the Gospel again?" Kay echoed.

"You've shown me that I've got to have a Savior, Kay. I've only been kidding myself when I said that I didn't need Christ. Would you explain to me about salvation again?"

"Of course, I will, Marilyn," the missionary's daughter said.

THE
DANNY ORLIS
SERIES

The Danny Orlis series, by Bernard Palmer, delivers a blend of adventure, mystery, and suspense through various settings—from the Canadian wilderness to Guatemalan jungles. Danny Orlis, an adept outdoorsman, skilled athlete, and committed Christian, employs his quick thinking, calm bravery, and biblical solutions to confront everyday problems and hair-raising dangers. Early stories focus on Danny navigating school life, sports, and outdoor challenges, while in later books, Danny and his wife Kay provide wisdom and guidance to youngsters facing lifelike situations and challenges. Having sold over two million copies, this series has made Palmer a renowned author in Christian youth literature. Palmer is also the author of the Felicia Cartright series and various other series for Christian youth.

AVAILABLE FROM WWW.ANEKOPRESS.COM